Penguin Books

Debbie Go Home

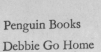

Alan Paton was born at Pietermaritzburg, Natal, in 1903.
He attended Pietermaritzburg College, at which he
afterwards taught, and the Natal University College, at
which he took his B.Sc. degree in Mathematics and
Physics and the Diploma of Education. In 1925 he went
to teach in Ixopo, where *Cry, the Beloved Country* opens.
A few years later he became Principal of Diepkloof
Reformatory for delinquent African lads in Johannesburg,
where he set out to introduce a system of graduated
freedom, and transformed it from a prison to a school.
Before writing this book Alan Paton wrote numerous
articles on South African problems for national
periodicals, and this he continues to do. His latest
publication is *Apartheid and the Archbishop* (1973).

Penguins have also published his novels *Debbie Go
Home* and *Too Late the Phalarope*, and he is represented in
two Penguin anthologies, *South African Writing Today*
and *The Penguin Book of South African Verse*.

He was National President of the Liberal Party in South
Africa until its disbandment, under persistent official
pressure, in May 1968. He holds honorary degrees from
Yale University, Kenyon College, Harvard, Rhodes,
Natal, Trent and Edinburgh, and in 1960 he received the
Freedom House Award (U.S.A.).

Alan Paton, who has two sons, lives in Natal.

Debbie Go Home

Alan Paton

Penguin Books
in association with Jonathan Cape

Penguin Books Ltd, Harmondsworth,
Middlesex, England
Penguin Books, 625 Madison Avenue,
New York, New York 10022, U.S.A.
Penguin Books Australia Ltd, Ringwood,
Victoria, Australia
Penguin Books Canada Ltd, 41 Steelcase Road West,
Markham, Ontario, Canada
Penguin Books (N.Z.) Ltd, 182-190 Wairau Road,
Auckland 10, New Zealand

First published by Jonathan Cape 1961
Published in Penguin Books 1965
Reprinted 1968, 1972, 1977

Made and printed in Great Britain by
Hazell Watson & Viney Ltd,
Aylesbury, Bucks
Set in Monotype Garamond

Contents

Debbie Go Home

It was too late to do anything or hide anything. There was the front gate clicking and Jim de Villiers walking up the path, one hour before his time. The room was strewn with paper and pins, and there was Janie in the new white dress, that cost more than any dress had ever cost in that house, or in most other houses that they knew.

Janie was in a panic because she saw her father walking up the front path, an hour before his time. She was a docile child, and obeyed her father in almost everything. Now she and her mother were deceiving him, and they were going to be caught in the act. She wanted to run, hide, cry, anything but stand there and wait.

Mrs de Villiers saw that her daughter was in a panic, wringing her hands and wanting to run and hide. 'Stand still,' she said sharply. 'It was my doing, and I'll take the medicine. And don't talk unless your father orders you to.'

Then Jim de Villiers opened the front door that led immediately into the combined living-, dining-, sitting-room of the small house. He was angry at once. It didn't look good to see your daughter in a panic because you got home unexpectedly. It didn't look good to see your wife standing on guard, assuming already that you were going to attack her and her daughter. It didn't look good any-how to see that you had stumbled on a secret that wasn't meant for you. What if one of his friends had been with him? That would have been a fine thing to see.

He put down his hat and his lunch tin, and then he looked at the scene, daughter being fitted by mother into a dress of some stuff all shining and silver. Then, because no one would speak, he had to say, 'What's all this about?'

'It's a dress, Jim,' said his wife. Some other time he could have laughed, not now, with the whole thing hanging over him. But she didn't wait for him to laugh or not to laugh. She went on as though she had learned a speech in the minute that it took him from the gate to the door.

'It's the first Debutantes' Ball,' she said, 'and it's going to be next month in the City Hall. Our girls are going to be received by the Administrator and his wife. I didn't think you'd like it, Jim, so I thought we wouldn't tell you.'

'Why didn't you think I wouldn't like it?' he asked, purposely obtuse. 'I've nothing against a ball.'

She didn't answer him, so he said, 'Who's organizing it?'

'The Parkside Mothers' Club, Jim.'

De Villiers sat down. 'The Parkside Mothers' Club, eh? But what about the Parkside fathers? Are you making fools of them all?'

'They don't hold your views, Jim.'

'They don't,' he agreed. 'If they did, we shouldn't be outcasts in the country where we were born.'

He returned to his attack. 'Why did you think I'd be against the ball?' he asked.

He watched her stonily, and he looked at his daughter too, but she didn't look at him.

'Shall I tell you why?' he said, and when she didn't answer, he said again, 'Shall I tell you why?' So that she replied unwillingly, 'Yes, you tell me why.'

He went to the job with satisfaction.

'You've got some high white folks to receive our girls,' he said. 'They'll smile at them and shake their hands, and

the Administrator will talk a lot of shit about the brotherhood of man and the sisterhood of women. But if one of
our girls went to his house next week, it would be to the
back door.'

He looked at his daughter and said to her angrily,
'Haven't you got any pride? Why can't you be what you
are, instead of what the white people think you ought to
be? They don't think you're good enough to shake hands
with them, but for the sake of this brotherhood shit you're
allowed to shake hands with the Administrator. I suppose
you're proud of that.'

He continued to look at Janie, but she would not look
at him.

'Talk to me, Jim,' said his wife pleadingly. 'I got her
into this.'

The girl came to life.

'You didn't,' she said. 'I wanted to be presented from
the time I first heard.'

'Shut your bloody mouth,' her father shouted at her.
'You don't belong to the Parkside Mothers' Club, do
you?'

He turned to his wife. 'I'll talk to you,' he said. 'You
want our girls to be received by the Administrator, do
you? Received into what? Into a world where they take
away your vote and your house. Do you need a white
Administrator to do that? How can a white man receive
you into our kind of world? And why the hell should he?'

His anger was overpowering him and he stood up.

'Who made him Administrator?' he shouted. 'The
Government, the same bloody Government that took
away our votes and our houses, and can make me a black
man tomorrow if they feel like it. So you get their man to
come and receive our daughters at a ball?'

He rounded on his daughter.

'Wait till your brother gets back from the university,' he said. 'Tell him you're going to a Debutantes' Ball, and a white man is going to welcome you into the shitting world that he and his friends have made for you. What do you think he'll have to say?'

He put his head in his hands in such a way that his wife called out, 'Jim, Jim,' and took a step towards him.

'Don't touch me,' he said. 'It's you who's driving me mad, licking the hand that whips us. Making me ashamed of all coloured people.'

Mother and daughter watched him anxiously, but he suddenly pulled himself together.

'Where did you get the money for the dress?' he asked. 'From what I give you?'

'No, Jim. I sewed for it.'

'How much was it?'

'Four pounds.'

He spoke to his daughter. 'Take it off,' he said. 'And never put it on again.' He sat down again, trembling a little.

Janie looked at her mother.

'Go to your room and take it off,' said her mother, 'and stay there till you're called.'

When her daughter had gone she said, 'Jim, go and lie down.'

'Lie down? What for?'

'You're sick.'

'Yes, I'm sick all right, of all this belly-creeping to the same people that take away our rights.'

She shook her head at him.

'Why are you home early?' she asked.

She knew him well. He could never hide anything, it all

showed in his face. Something was badly wrong. When something was wrong, all the heart went out of him.

'There's trouble at the factory,' she said.

He put his head in his hands again, this time covering his face. She went and stood by him, and said to him, 'Have they put you off?'

He shook his head. 'Not yet,' he said.

'When will they put you off?'

'We don't know. It's not certain yet.'

'What's the matter? Is the market bad?'

'No.'

'Jim, I can't hear you, speaking through your hands like that.' She took his hands away from his face, and knelt down by him, holding them.

'Are they dissatisfied, Jim?'

'No.'

'Do they say you're too old?'

'No.'

Baffled, she searched his face. He had brought bad news, but he couldn't tell.

'Jim, you must tell me. I *must* know.'

Then it came, seeming to tear at him as it came out.

'It's a new law,' he said hoarsely. 'A new law. The Industrial Conciliation Act.'

'What does it say, Jim?'

' It says the Minister can reserve any occupation. So we may have to go. We, we. The Coloured men.'

She jumped to her feet. 'The wickedness,' she said. 'Oh the wickedness!'

She had no more to say, nor he, until she asked him again, 'Why did you come home early, Jim?'

'I was sick,' he said. 'Just plain sick. I seemed to bring up all the food I ever ate. The boss said, what's the matter,

Jim? I said it just made me sick to hear there was such a law.'

'The wickedness,' she said. 'Oh the wickedness!'

'The boss said, Jim, it's not my fault. I said to him, you're white, aren't you? So he went away.'

Suddenly he shouted at her.

'I suppose you think I did wrong. I suppose you think I should of got down on my belly and licked his hand.'

'No, Jim, I would never have wanted that.'

'But you want your daughter to shake their hands, and curtsy to them, and be received into their bloody world?'

'That's why!' she said. 'There's many a hard thing coming to her as well. I'd like her to have one night, in a nice dress and the coloured lights, dancing before the Administrator in the City Hall. We get kicks aplenty. I wanted her to have a boost. And for one night the young men will be wearing gloves, and bowing to her as gentlemanly as you like, not pawing at her in some dark yard.'

'It was good enough for us,' he said.

'You never pawed at me,' she said. 'But don't you want it to be better for her? Don't you want her to begin where you left off?'

'Where I left off?' he asked. 'Where did I leave off? With a law that took away my job, and a law that took away my vote, and a law that's going to take away my house, all because I've a coloured skin? Can't you see it's going to be worse for her?'

'That may be,' she said. 'That's more reason I want her to have just this one night. Jim, go and lie down. I'll bring you a cup of tea.'

He got to his feet.

'All right, I'll go,' he said. Then perhaps he thought he was being too obedient. He said, 'You go and comfort the debutante.'

He went into their bedroom and shut the door, and she sat down and put her head in her hands too, not so much hopelessly because she was never hopeless, but because she couldn't see a way out of this hopeless mess. She sat there thinking for a long time, till a voice said to her, 'What's got you down, Ma?'

'Nothing's got me down,' she said, 'not yet. Johnny, how long have you been home?'

'Quite a time,' said Johnny, 'quite a time.'

He was a gum-chewing nonchalant, and one of the militant students at the university.

'How many things have you heard?' she asked. 'One or two?'

'Two.'

'What are they?'

'The lost job,' he said. 'And the lost ball.'

'And the lost mother,' she said, 'who doesn't know what to do. But it's your father I worry about.'

'He hopes too much,' said Johnny. 'He knows what the world is like, yet he goes on hoping. And when the blow comes, it knocks him down.'

'Don't you hope?' she asked.

'I hope?' he said. He laughed with worldly wisdom. 'I hope for nothing,' he said fiercely. 'Nothing, nothing, nothing. I hope for nothing that I won't get my own way.' He laughed again. 'You ought to be pleased that I'm that way,' he said. 'What does the Bible say? Blessed is he who hopes for nothing, for he shall not be disappointed.'

'The Bible doesn't say that,' she said.

He shrugged his shoulders.

'How would I know? But even if the Bible doesn't say it, it's God's own truth.'

'Johnny, you've got to help. You can think what you like, believe what you like. But you've got to help me to get Janie to that ball.'

His face turned ugly.

'To be received by the Administrator,' he said. 'Not me.'

'I know what you say,' she said. 'That he's white. I know he's white too. But the night of the ball he's the Administrator, he's not white any more, he's got no colour.'

'He's always got colour for me,' said Johnny. 'A dirty stinking white. And I'll help no sister of mine to shake his hand. Can you see the sense of it? It's not the ordinary people we're allowed to shake hands with, only the big shots. How does that make sense to you?'

'It makes sense to me,' she said pleadingly. 'He's the Administrator, he belongs to us all.' She waved him quiet. 'Give me a chance to speak,' she said. 'I know we didn't elect him or appoint him,' she said, 'but in a way he's above all colour. But that's not my argument, Johnny . . .'

'I know your argument,' he said. 'You want her to have one night, one night of magic and romance. You want her to go in a shining silver dress, like the Duchess of Musgrave Road.' He parodied her argument without pity. 'She'll get kicks, poor little girl, and they'll take something more away from her when she grows up, and they'll call her a tottie and think that she'd sell herself for a bottle of gin, but this one night – just this one night – let them treat her like a queen.'

The boy was pouring it out hot and strong, till he

looked at his mother, and saw that she had put her head in her hands again. He lost his enthusiasm at once, and said to her, 'Why should I help you for that?'

She didn't lift her head, but she said to him, 'Because I'm your mother, because it's your mother wants this one thing, this one harmless thing.'

There was a knock at the door, and she said to him in a whisper, 'I can't face a visitor, make some excuse.' Then he saw that she was afraid of weeping. He opened the door, and went out quickly, but in a minute he was back. His mother was wiping her eyes, and she said to him, 'Who was it?'

'Someone wanting the Tomlinsons,' he said.

He stood and looked at her, and remembered a thousand acts of love. He went to her and said, 'Don't cry, Ma, I'll do it for you. This once, and never again.'

'I shan't want it again,' she said. 'Only this once.'

He threw up his eyes to heaven piously. 'Only this once,' he said in a false high voice, 'let her be treated like a queen.'

She blew her nose and laughed.

'Tell your father, I'm making the tea,' she said.

'I hope this won't get you into trouble with the Unity Movement, Johnny.'

'That would no doubt cause you grief and pain,' he said.

'I can't say that,' she said, 'but I don't want trouble for you.'

'I'll look after myself,' he said, chewing his gum.

He went to his parents' bedroom and knocked on the door. His father said, 'Come in,' and there he was lying on the bed.

'Have a cigarette, Dad.'

'Thanks, Johnny, don't mind if I do.'

'Smoke while you can,' advised his son cynically. 'Ma's told me about the job. Has it got you down?'

'Yes, son,' said his father apologetically. 'For the time it's got me down.'

'It's because you hope for the best and fear for the worst,' said his son. 'I expect the worst, so when it comes, I don't take it hard.'

'You were lucky,' said his father defensively. 'I was brought up in a world where we always hoped for the best. But you live in a time when no false hopes are left. I was a Smuts man, don't forget.'

'Smuts,' said Johnny contemptuously. 'Who was Smuts?'

'Johnny,' said his father, 'you see me down now, but I want to be up tomorrow. I want to speak at the union meeting. Will you help me with a speech?'

'A hard speech?'

Jim de Villiers considered it.

'I want a fighting speech,' he said. 'I want to stand up for our rights, but I don't want to blackguard the whites. I don't want trouble, Johnny.'

'You don't, eh? Then why don't you let Janie go to the ball?'

Jim looked at his son. 'I don't get you,' he said. 'Are you wanting Janie to go to the ball?'

Johnny chewed his gum. '*I* don't want her to go to the ball,' he said carelessly. 'But her going to the ball is the price of a speech.'

His father sat up on the bed. 'Do I hear you right?' he asked.

'You hear me right,' said Johnny. 'It's the price for a fighting speech, free of all hatred, bitterness, resentment, full of shit about freedom and the rights of man. No one will give you a better.'

'Why are you doing this, Johnny?'

Johnny chewed his gum. 'Because Ma said to me, I'm your mother,' he said. 'And your mother wants your sister to have a night as a queen.'

He looked at his father with expressionless eyes.

His father said, 'I don't understand you, Johnny.'

'You don't have to understand me,' said Johnny. 'You just have to tell me, is she going to the ball?'

'I don't understand you, Johnny. It was mainly because of you that I said she couldn't go.'

'Now it'll be mainly because of me that you'll say she can go,' said Johnny.

Jim de Villiers lay down again. 'You beat me,' he said.

'I beat lots of people,' said his son, 'Just tell me, can she go, so I can get on with the speech.'

'All right, she can go,' he said, 'on one condition. Tell me how you justify it.'

'Rock-bottom necessity,' said Johnny. 'If I boycott American food, and I'm dying of hunger, and everywhere round me is American food, then I eat American food.'

'You eat American food so you can go on boycotting it,' said de Villiers.

Johnny smiled against his will. 'You're getting better,' he said. 'Listen, Dad, I can't study in a house of weeping women.'

'Was your mother weeping?'

'As near as she gets.'

'Son, don't tell her we bargained for it.'

'O.K. I won't. See you again.'

He went to his room, which was no more than a bit of enclosed veranda, and sat down at his small table to think about the speech on freedom and the rights of man. Then on second thoughts he got up, and hauled some posters out from under his bed and put them against the wall where they could be seen. They were all headed 'DEBU-TANTES BALL'. One said, 'DEBBIE GO HOME', and another, ornamented with a bar of music, asked, 'WHO STOLE MY VOTE AWAY?' The third one was his own, but his friends thought it was too learned, for it said, 'WEL-COME, SPICK LITTLE LICKSPITTLE.' When he had put them up, he sat down at the table, but his thoughts were not on the speech, they were on his mother's entrance.

Then she burst in, with her eyes shining, and she would have embraced him if she had not suddenly seen the new decorations.

'I suppose you came to thank me,' he said.

'I did.'

She sat down in the other chair, and looked at the posters.

'You can't do that now,' she said.

'Why not?'

'You can't,' she said. 'You can't give with one hand, and take away with the other.'

'I gave you your share,' he said hotly. 'That's my share there.'

'You can't do it,' she said. 'If you take your share, mine's worth nothing. Do you think that's fair?'

'I can't help it,' he said. 'We fixed this up long before I knew you wanted Janie to go.' When she said nothing, he went on, 'What we're doing is an important thing. You can't just stop because your sister's going to a ball.'

'I understand what you're doing,' she said. 'I understand what you want, you and your friends. But don't you ever let up? Don't you ever have mercy on anyone?'

'Mercy,' he said, with a sudden flight of fancy, 'it's like a door of a cage. Open it once, and everything's gone.'

'Do you know Hazel's going to the ball?' she asked.

'Yes,' he said defiantly.

'What about Fred?' she asked. 'Is he acting the same way as you?'

'Yes.'

'The world's mad,' she said. She stood up and rubbed her brow with the back of her hand. 'Brother against sister, husband against wife. You know what Christ said?'

He looked at her with annoyance. She took an unfair advantage of him by talking religion. He could sneer at white people's religion, but not at hers.

'Go your own way,' she said. 'But let me teach you one thing about giving. When you give, give with your whole heart. Don't keep half of it back.'

She went out and closed his door. As all his attention had been on her entrance, now it was on her exit. He heard no doors opening, no voices speaking. The house was quite silent. When he could stand it no more he followed her, and found her sitting in the living-room, in the evening dark.

'What are you doing?' he asked.

She answered him in a matter-of-fact voice. That was her way, that was why you had to live your life with her to know what she was.

'I'm thinking it out,' she said.

She didn't ask for help, he knew she wouldn't ask for any. A spiritless husband, a day-dreaming daughter, a tough son, they weren't much use to her.

'If it'll help you,' he said, 'I won't let Janie see me.'

She considered his proposition. 'How will you do

that?' she asked. 'You know where the cars will stop, outside the main foyer. Where will you be, inside or out?'

'Wouldn't you like to know?' he asked. 'All I'm saying is, I won't let Janie see me.'

'Is Fred doing the same for Hazel?' she asked.

He could not help admiring her cleverness.

'That's Fred's business,' he said.

She got up and he saw that she was intending to kiss him, so he waved her away.

'Don't thank me too much,' he said harshly. 'She'll see all the others.'

But she kissed him all the same.

'Give the kiss to Fred,' she said. 'Now I'll go and tell Janie the news.'

At Janie's door she turned and gave him a smile.

'You'd better get on with your father's speech,' she said.

Ha'penny

Of the six hundred boys at the reformatory, about one hundred were from ten to fourteen years of age. My Department had from time to time expressed the intention of taking them away, and of establishing a special institution for them, more like an industrial school than a reformatory. This would have been a good thing, for their offences were very trivial, and they would have been better by themselves. Had such a school been established, I should have liked to be Principal of it myself, for it would have been an easier job; small boys turn instinctively towards affection, and one controls them by it, naturally and easily.

Some of them, if I came near them, either on parade or in school or at football, would observe me watchfully, not directly or fully, but obliquely and secretly; sometimes I would surprise them at it, and make some small sign of recognition, which would satisfy them so that they would cease to observe me, and would give their full attention to the event of the moment. But I knew that my authority was thus confirmed and strengthened.

The secret relations with them were a source of continuous pleasure to me. Had they been my own children I would no doubt have given a greater expression to it. But often I would move through the silent and orderly parade, and stand by one of them. He would look straight in front of him with a little frown of concentration that expressed both childish awareness of and manly indifference to my nearness. Sometimes I would tweak his ear, and he would give me a brief smile of acknowledgement, or frown with still greater concentration. It was natural, I suppose, to confine these outward expressions to the very smallest, but they were taken as symbolic, and some older boys would observe them and take themselves to be included. It was a relief, when the reformatory was passing through times of turbulence and trouble, and when there was danger of estrangement between authority and boys, to make these simple and natural gestures, which were reassurances to both me and them that nothing important had changed.

On Sunday afternoons when I was on duty I would take my car to the reformatory and watch the free boys being signed out at the gate. This simple operation was also watched by many boys not free, who would tell each other, 'In so many weeks I'll be signed out myself.' Among the watchers were always some of the small boys, and these I would take by turns in the car. We would go out to the Potchefstroom Road with its ceaseless stream of traffic, and to the Baragwanath crossroads, and come back by the Van Wyksrus road to the reformatory. I would talk to them about their families, their parents, their sisters and brothers, and I would pretend to know nothing of Durban, Port Elizabeth, Potchefstroom, and Clocolan, and ask them if these places were bigger than Johannesburg.

One of the small boys was Ha'penny, and he was about twelve years old. He came from Bloemfontein and was the biggest talker of them all. His mother worked in a white person's house, and he had two brothers and two sisters. His brothers were Richard and Dickie, and his sisters Anna and Mina.

'Richard and Dickie?' I asked.

'Yes, meneer.'

'In English,' I said, 'Richard and Dickie are the same name.'

When we returned to the reformatory, I sent for Ha'penny's papers; there it was plainly set down, Ha'-penny was a waif, with no relatives at all. He had been taken in from one home to another, but he was naughty and uncontrollable, and eventually had taken to pilfering at the market.

I then sent for the Letter Book, and found that Ha'penny wrote regularly, or rather that others wrote for him till he could write himself, to Mrs Betty Maarman, of 48 Vlak Street, Bloemfontein. But Mrs Maarman had never once replied to him. When questioned, he had said, perhaps she is sick. I sat down and wrote at once to the Social Welfare Officer at Bloemfontein, asking him to investigate.

The next time I had Ha'penny out in the car I questioned him again about his family. And he told me the same as before, his mother, Richard and Dickie, Anna and Mina. But he softened the 'D' of Dickie, so that it sounded now like Tickie.

'I thought you said Dickie,' I said.

'I said Tickie,' he said.

He watched me with concealed apprehension, and I came to the conclusion that this waif of Bloemfontein was a clever boy, who had told me a story that was all imagination, and had changed one single letter of it to make it safe from any question. And I thought I understood it all too, that he was ashamed of being without a family and had invented them all, so that no one might discover that he was fatherless and motherless and that no one in the world cared whether he was alive or dead. This gave me a strong feeling for him, and I went out of my way to manifest towards him that fatherly care that the State, though not in those words, had enjoined upon me by giving me this job.

Then the letter came from the Social Welfare Officer in Bloemfontein, saying that Mrs Betty Maarman of 48 Vlak Street was a real person, and that she had four children, Richard and Dickie, Anna and Mina, but that Ha'penny was no child of hers, and she knew him only as a derelict of the streets. She had never answered his letters, because he wrote to her as 'Mother', and she was no mother of his, nor did she wish to play any such role. She was a decent woman, a faithful member of the church, and she had no thought of corrupting her family by letting them have anything to do with such a child.

But Ha'penny seemed to me anything but the usual delinquent; his desire to have a family was so strong, and his reformatory record was so blameless, and his anxiety to please and obey so great, that I began to feel a great duty towards him. Therefore I asked him about his 'mother'.

He could not speak enough of her, nor with too high praise. She was loving, honest, and strict. Her home was clean. She had affection for all her children. It was clear that the homeless child, even as he had attached himself to me, would have attached himself to her; he had observed her even as he had observed me, but did not know the secret of how to open her heart, so that she would take him in, and save him from the lonely life that he led.

'Why did you steal when you had such a mother?' I asked.

He could not answer that; not all his brains nor his courage could find an answer to such a question, for he knew that with such a mother he would not have stolen at all.

'The boy's name is Dickie,' I said, 'not Tickie.'

And then he knew the deception was revealed. Another boy might have said, 'I told you it was Dickie', but he was too intelligent for that; he knew that if I had established that the boy's name was Dickie, I must have established other things too. I was shocked by the immediate and visible effect of my action. His whole brave assurance died within him, and he stood there exposed, not as a liar, but as a homeless child who had surrounded himself with mother, brothers, and sisters, who did not exist. I had shattered the very foundations of his pride, and his sense of human significance.

He fell sick at once, and the doctor said it was tuberculosis. I wrote at once to Mrs Maarman, telling her the whole story, of how this small boy had observed her, and had decided that she was the person he desired for his mother. But she wrote back saying that she could take no responsibility for him. For one thing, Ha'penny was a Mosuto, and she was a coloured woman; for another, she had never had a child in trouble, and how could she take such a boy?

Tuberculosis is a strange thing; sometimes it manifests itself suddenly in the most unlikely host, and swiftly sweeps to the end. Ha'penny withdrew himself from the world, from all Principals and mothers, and the doctor said there was little hope. In desperation I sent money for Mrs Maarman to come.

She was a decent, homely woman, and seeing that the situation was serious, she, without fuss or embarrassment, adopted Ha'penny for her own. The whole reformatory accepted her as his mother. She sat the whole day with him, and talked to him of Richard and Dickie, Anna and Mina, and how they were all waiting for him to come home. She poured out her affection on him, and had no fear of his sickness, nor did she allow it to prevent her from satisfying his hunger to be owned. She talked to him of what they would do when he came back, and how he would go to the school, and what they would buy for Guy Fawkes night.

He in his turn gave his whole attention to her, and when I visited him he was grateful, but I had passed out of his world. I felt judged in that I had sensed only the existence and not the measure of his desire. I wished I had done something sooner, more wise, more prodigal.

We buried him on the reformatory farm, and Mrs Maarman said to me, 'When you put up the cross, put he was my son.

'I'm ashamed,' she said, 'that I wouldn't take him.'

'The sickness,' I said, 'the sickness would have come.'

'No,' she said, shaking her head with certainty. 'It wouldn't have come. And if it had come at home, it would have been different.'

So she left for Bloemfontein, after her strange visit to a reformatory. And I was left too, with the resolve to be more prodigal in the task that the State, though not in so many words, had enjoined on me.

The Divided House

Of all the boys at the reformatory, Jacky was one of the strangest. He had once been a Pondo of Pondoland, but the big city was now in his blood. He was a closed-up, reserved kind of boy, and had no close companions; but he enjoyed a kind of popularity none the less, for he played a magnificent game of football. We gave him his freedom because no one knew much about him, not even the Tailoring Instructor who had worked with him for months. Of every hundred boys we made free, three absconded at once, the first time they were allowed to roam about the farm on their own. But another three had a conscience, and absconded only on the second or fifth or seventh occasion. Jacky was one of these, and one Sunday afternoon he failed to report back at five o'clock.

Some days after, I was visiting some boys who had been temporarily transferred to the non-European hospital, and whom should I see in one of the wards, with an African constable sitting guard over him, but Jacky. I told the constable he was one of my boys, and asked if I might speak to him.

'What are you doing here, Jacky?'

He looked at me shamefacedly.

'I was shot, father,' he said.

'How did you get shot?'

'I was breaking into a house, father.'

Of course Jacky lost his freedom when the magistrate returned him to the reformatory, and he went back to the main building. But he was such a good tailor that he was allowed to return to his old work. When he had been back for a short time, he asked to see me, and the Tailoring Instructor brought him in.

'Jacky has a story to tell the Principal,' he said, and then he looked at me apologetically. 'It's a strange story,' he said.

'Well, Jacky?'

'When I was in hospital, father, a voice spoke to me.'

'A voice? What voice?'

'God's voice, father.'

'And what did he say?'

'He said, "Jacky, you won't die, your work is not yet finished."'

'And what did you say?'

'I said, "Father, what is the work?"'

'Yes?'

'And he said, "Jacky, I want you to be a priest."'

I sat and considered it, and then I said to him, 'That's a new kind of work for you.'

If there was any irony, he took no notice.

'It's a new kind of work,' he said.

'How far have you been in school, Jacky?'

'Standard Four, father.'

'A priest has to go further than that.'

'I'm ready,' he said.

'You're asking,' I said, 'to go to the school?'

'Yes, father.'

'Then you can go to the school.'

So Jacky was put in Standard Five in the school, and though not brilliant, he worked hard and well.

In a few days he was back with the Head Teacher.

'What is it, Jacky?'

'Father, I am asking to go back to the free hostels.'

'Absconders don't go back to the free hostels,' I said. 'They go back to the main building.'

'I know,' he said, 'but I can't pray and study in the main building. There's too much noise.'

I knew that Jacky was spending much time in prayer and study, when he wasn't playing football.

'You can go back to the hostels,' I said. 'Are you in earnest, Jacky?'

'I'm in earnest, father. I am determined to be a priest.'

So Jacky went back to the hostels. He was an exemplary character, quiet and obedient, and spent much time by himself, praying and reading. The most extraordinary outward change was in his bodily cleanliness; he looked wholesome, and his face was shining. He washed and ironed his clothes every few days, which was really against the rules. He made more progress in school than his intelligence promised, and asked if he could preach in the hostels, where he had a small band of disciples. There was nothing extreme about it, for he spoke quietly of his own conversion, and asked others to follow his example before it was too late; in the meantime he went on playing his magnificent football. So he continued for some months, and it appeared that some deep change had taken place in his life, and that he thought nothing of the long period of training that stretched out before him, so long as he could become a priest.

Therefore it was a disappointment when he failed one day to appear at the evening parade of all free boys. The Head Teacher brought him to me.

'Why were you not at parade, Jacky?'

'It was the voice,' he said.

'What did it tell you, Jacky?'

35

'It told me to go and pray, father.'

'Where?'

'Down at the trees by the stables.'

'A priest must obey the laws,' I said.

'I know, father.'

'Therefore,' I said, 'if this voice tells you again to go and pray, you will go at once and ask your teacher's permission.'

'I promise it, father.'

So Jacky continued again for some months, washing and ironing his clothes, working hard at school, playing hard at football, and preaching once a week at the hostels. Then he failed again to appear at the parade. The Head Teacher sent at once to the trees by the stables, but no Jacky was there.

'Have you thought, sir,' asked the Head Teacher diffidently, 'that he might be smoking *dagga*?'

Now although the smoking of *dagga* is common in our cities, and although it is one of the great reformatory enemies, I was shaken, and said, 'What makes you think that?'

'Sometimes his manner is strange,' he said.

And that of course is the great sign, after the smell of the weed itself; for the humble come out with sudden insolence, and the obedient with sudden disobedience, the open-hearted become secretive, the gay sullen.

The next morning he brought Jacky to me.

'Well, Jacky?'

'Father?'

'Where were you yesterday?'

'In the trees by the stables, father.'

'Praying?'

'Yes, father.'

I looked him in the eyes for some time, but he could not endure it.

'Jacky.'

'Yes, father.'

'We searched in the trees by the stables.'

He did not maintain that we had searched inefficiently, nor did he pretend that he was in some other trees. He watched me anxiously, almost humbly.

'Would you lie to me?' I asked.

And he said in a subdued voice, 'No, father.'

'Have you been smoking *dagga*?'

He winced. The question was a hard blow to him. He would not look at me, but kept his eyes on the ground.

'Answer me, Jacky.'

'I smoked it,' he said.

I was silent a long time, so that he might feel that his admission had shocked me.

'You want to be a priest?'

'Yes, father.'

'You want to be a priest,' I said, 'and you want to smoke *dagga* also.'

My voice rose, and he turned his face away from me.

'But it cannot be done,' I said.

He looked at me with anguish.

'You are forcing me,' I said, 'you are forcing me to take away your freedom and send you to some other job.'

'No, no,' he said. He dropped on his knees in the office and began to pray silently. It was a strange thing to be there. When he was finished, he rose and said to me earnestly, 'I do not want to smoke *dagga*.'

'How many more chances do you want?' I said.

'One, father.'

'You can have it,' I said.

Yet of all reformatory enemies, *dagga* is the most insidious. It tempts free boys to break bounds, and to go seeking it in Pimville, Kliptown, and Orlando. It tempts them to steal goods, especially clothes, which they trade for the terrible weed. And Jacky's next offence was to steal a jacket from one of the hostels, and to sell it in Orlando. So he was brought to me again. But this time it was a Special Court, which we used when we wished to bring home to a boy the gravity of an offence. The Principal and the Vice-Principal were there, and the Chief Supervisor, the African Head Teacher, and the Tailoring Instructor. When Jacky came in, he was shocked to see us all.

He pleaded guilty to the offences of theft and buying *dagga*, so that there was nothing to do but to decide how to deal with him. After the long discussion I said to him, 'The Court does not say you cannot be a priest. But it says you must go back to the main building, and lose your freedom, and that you must go back to your tailoring. Yet if you are after some time still determined to be a priest, you will be allowed to return to the hostels and the school.'

Jacky looked at us as though he could not believe it, as though he could not believe in such a punishment. He could not speak, and it was uncomfortable to look at him.

'The football,' said Jacky, hoarsely.

'What about the football, Jacky?'

'Couldn't you take away the football?' he said. 'Couldn't you take the freedom? But not the school, not the school.'

It was painful to listen to him, so I looked at my fellow judges, but, like judges, they were impassive. Left to ourselves, we might have done something; left to myself, I might have done something. But I had asked them to judge, and I could not speak first; and I was the Principal, so perhaps they felt they could not speak first either. So society and the law were not moved. Jacky was taken away, the thief recompensed, the priest defeated.

*

Shortly afterwards Jacky attacked the head-boy of the Tailor's Shop with a pair of scissors, and escaped into the trees. He was arrested in Pretoria for house-breaking, but this time he was sent to prison for six months. I had a letter from him there, repenting of all past follies, and saying that he was still determined to be a priest. The letter was earnest and penitent, and I had no doubt that the struggle was still being waged; therefore I answered with words of encouragement, telling him that he could come back to us if he wished. Yet I knew that the boy who wrote the letter would, so far as men knew, always be defeated, till one day he would give up both hope and ghost, and leave to his enemy the sole tenancy of the divided house.

Life for a Life

The doctor had closed up the ugly hole in Flip's skull so that his widow, and her brothers and sisters, and their wives and husbands and children, and Flip's own brothers and sisters and their wives and husbands and children, could come and stand for a minute and look down on the hard stony face of the master of Kroon, one of the richest farmers of the whole Karroo. The cars kept coming and going, the police, the doctor, the newspapermen, the neighbours from near and far.

All the white women were in the house, and all the white men outside. An event like this, the violent death of one of themselves, drew them together in an instant, so that all the world might see that they were one, and that they would not rest till justice had been done. It was this standing there, this drawing together, that kept the brown people in their small stone houses, talking in low voices; and their fear communicated itself to their children, so that there was no need to silence them. Now and then one of them would leave the houses to relieve his needs in the bushes, but otherwise there was no movement on this side of the valley. Each family sat in its house, at a little distance from each front door, watching with anxious fascination the goings and the comings of the white people standing in front of the big house.

Then the white predikant came from Poort, you could tell him by the black hat and the black clothes. He shook hands with Big Baas Flip's sons, and said words of comfort to them. Then all the men followed him into the house, and after a while the sound of the slow determined singing was carried across the valley, to the small stone houses on the other side, to Enoch Maarman, head shepherd of Kroon, and his wife Sara, sitting just inside the door of their own house. Maarman's anxiety showed itself in the movements of his face and hands, and his wife knew of his condition but kept her face averted from it. Guilt lay heavily upon them both, because they had hated Big Baas Flip, not with clenched fists and bared teeth, but, as befitted people in their station, with salutes and deference.

Sara suddenly sat erect.

'They are coming,' she said.

They watched the four men leave the big stone house, and take the path that led to the small stone houses, and both could feel the fear rising in them. Their guilt weighed down on them all the more heavily because they felt no grief. They felt all the more afraid because the show of grief might have softened the harshness of the approaching ordeal. Someone must pay for so terrible a crime, and if not the one who did it, then who better than the one who could not grieve? That morning Maarman had stood hat in hand before Baas Gysbert, who was Big Baas Flip's eldest son, and had said to him, 'My people are sorry to hear of this terrible thing.' And Baas Gysbert had given him the terrible answer, 'That could be so.'

Then Sara said to him, 'Robbertse is one.'

He nodded. He knew that Robbertse was one, the big detective with the temper that got out of hand, so that reddish foam would come out of his mouth, and he would hold a man by the throat till one of his colleagues would shout at him to let the man go. Sara's father, who was one of the wisest men in all the district of Poort, said that he could never be sure whether Robbertse was mad or only pretending to be, but that it didn't really matter, because whichever it was, it was dangerous.

Maarman and his wife stood up when two of the detectives came to the door of the small stone house. One was Robbertse, but both were big men and confident. They wore smart sports jackets and grey flannels, and grey felt hats on their heads. They came in and kept their hats on their heads, looking round the small house with the air of masters. They spoke to each other as though there were nobody standing there waiting to be spoken to.

Then Robbertse said, 'You are Enoch Maarman?'

'Yes, baas.'

'The head shepherd?'

'Yes, baas.'

'Who are the other shepherds?'

Enoch gave him the names, and Robbertse sat down on one of the chairs, and wrote the names in his book. Then he tilted his hat back on his head and said, 'Has any of these men ever been in jail?'

Enoch moistened his lips. He wanted to say that the detective could easily find it out for himself, that he was the head shepherd and would answer any question about the farm or the work. But he said instead, 'I don't know, baas.'

'You don't know Kleinbooi was in jail at Christmas?'

'Yes, I know that, baas.'

Suddenly Robbertse was on his feet, and his head almost touching the ceiling, and his body almost filling the small room, and he was shouting in a tremendous voice, 'Then why did you lie?'

Sara had shrunk back into the wall, and was looking at

45

Robbertse out of terrified eyes, but Enoch did not move though he was deathly afraid.

He answered, 'I didn't mean to lie, baas. Kleinbooi was in jail for drink, not killing.'

Robbertse said, 'Killing? Why do you mention killing?'

Then when Enoch did not answer, the detective suddenly lifted his hand so that Enoch started back and knocked over the other chair. Down on his knees, and shielding his head with one hand, he set the chair straight again, saying, 'Baas, we know that you are here because the master was killed.'

But Robbertse's lifting his hand had been intended only to remove his hat from his head, and now with a grin he put his hat on the table.

'Why fall down,' he asked, 'because I take off my hat? I like to take off my hat in another man's house.'

He smiled at Sara, and looking at the chair now set upright, said to her, 'You can sit.'

When she made no attempt to sit on it, the smile left his face, and he said to her coldly and menacingly, 'You can sit.'

When she had sat down, he said to Maarman, 'Don't knock over any more chairs. For if one gets broken, you'll tell the magistrate I broke it, won't you? That I lifted it up and threatened you?'

'No, baas.'

Robbertse sat down again, and studied his book as though something were written there, not the names of shepherds. Then he said suddenly, out of nothing, 'You hated him, didn't you?'

And Enoch answered, 'No, baas.'

'Where's your son Johannes?'

'In Cape Town, baas.'

'Why didn't he become a shepherd?'

'I wouldn't let him, baas.'

'You sent him to the white university?'

'Yes, baas.'

'So that he could play the white baas?'

'No, baas.'

'Why does he never come to see you?'

'The Big Baas would not let him, baas.'

'Because he wouldn't become a shepherd?'

'Yes, baas.'

'So you hated him, didn't you?'

'No, baas.'

Robbertse looked at him with contempt.

'A man keeps your own son away from your door, because you want a better life for him, and you don't hate him? God, what are you made of?'

He continued to look at Maarman with contempt, then shrugged his shoulders as though it were a bad business; then he suddenly grew intimate, confidential, even friendly.

'Maarman, I have news for you, you may think it good, you may think it bad. But you have a right to know it, seeing it is about your son.'

The shepherd was suddenly filled with a new apprehension. Robbertse was preparing some new blow. That was the kind of man he was, he hated to see any coloured man holding his head up, he hated to see any coloured man anywhere but on his knees or his stomach.

'Your son,' said Robbertse, genially, 'you thought he was in Cape Town, didn't you?'

'Yes, baas.'

'Well, he isn't,' said Robbertse, 'he's here in Poort, he was seen there yesterday.'

47

He let it sink in, then he said to Maarman, 'He hated Big Baas Flip, didn't he?'

Maarman cried out, 'No, baas.'

For the second time Robbertse was on his feet, filling the room with his size, and his madness.

'He didn't hate him?' he shouted. 'God Almighty, Big Baas Flip wouldn't let him come to his own home, and see his own father and mother, but he didn't hate him. And you didn't hate him either, you creeping yellow bastard, what are you all made of?'

He looked at the shepherd out of his mad red eyes. Then with contempt he said again, 'You creeping yellow Hottentot bastard.'

'Baas,' said Maarman.

'What?'

'Baas, the baas can ask me what he likes, and I shall try to answer him, but I ask the baas not to insult me in my own house, before my own wife.'

Robbertse appeared delighted, charmed. Some other man might have been outraged that a coloured man should so advise him, but he was able to admire such manly pride.

'Insult you?' he said. 'Didn't you see me take off my hat when I came into this house?'

He turned to Sara and asked her, 'Didn't you see me take off my hat when I came into the house?'

'Yes, baas.'

'Did you think I was insulting your husband?'

'No, baas.'

Robbertse smiled at her ingratiatingly. 'I only called him a creeping yellow Hottentot bastard,' he said.

The cruel words destroyed the sense of piquancy for him, and now he was truly outraged. He took a step

48

towards the shepherd, and his colleague, the other detective, the silent one, suddenly shouted at him, 'Robbertse!'

Robbertse stopped. He looked vacantly at Maarman. 'Was someone calling me?' he asked. 'Did you hear a voice calling me?'

Maarman was terrified, fascinated, he could see the red foam. He was at a loss, not knowing whether this was madness, or madness affecting to be madness, or what it was.

'The other baas was calling you, baas.'

Then it was suddenly all over. Robbertse sat down again on the chair to ask more questions.

'You knew there was money stolen?'

'Yes, baas.'

'Who told you?'

'Mimi, the girl who works at the house.'

'You knew the money was in an iron safe, and they took it away?'

'Yes, baas.'

'Where would they take it to?'

'I don't know, baas.'

'Where would you have taken it, if you had stolen it?'

But Maarman didn't answer.

'You won't answer, eh?'

All three of them watched Robbertse anxiously, lest the storm should return. But he smiled benevolently at Maarman, as though he knew that even a coloured man must have pride, as though he thought all the better of him for it, and said, 'All right, I won't ask that question. But I want you to think of the places where that safe could be. It must have been carried by at least two men, perhaps more. And they couldn't have got it off the farm in the time. So it's still on the farm. Now all I want you to do is to think where it could be. No one knows this farm better than you.'

'I'll think, baas.'

The other detective suddenly said, 'The lieutenant's come.' The two of them stood just inside the door, looking over to the house on the other side of the valley. Then suddenly Robbertse rounded on Maarman, and catching him by the back of the neck, forced him to the door, so that he could look too.

'You see that,' he said. 'They want to know who killed Big Baas Flip, and they want to know soon. Do you see them?'

'Yes, baas.'

'And you see that lieutenant. He rides round in a Chrysler, and by God, he wants to know too. And by God he'll ride me if I don't find out.'

He pulled the shepherd back into the room, and put on his hat and went out, followed by the other.

'Don't think you've seen the last of me,' he said to Maarman. 'You've got to show me where your friends hid that safe.'

Then he and his companion joined the other two detectives, and all four of them turned back towards the big house. They talked animatedly, and more than once all of them stood for a moment while one of them made some point or put forward some theory. No one would have known that one of them was mad.

Twelve hours since they had taken her husband away. Twelve hours since the mad detective had come for him, with those red tormented eyes, as though the lieutenant were riding him too hard. He had grinned at her husband.

'Come and we'll look for the safe,' he said. The sun was sinking in the sky, over the hills of Kroon. It was not time to be looking for a safe.

She did not sleep that night. Her neighbours had come to sit with her, till midnight, till two o'clock, till four o'clock, but there was no sign. Why did he not come back? Were they still searching at this hour of the morning? Then the sun was rising, over the hills of Kroon.

On the other side of the valley the big house was awake, for this was the day that Big Baas Flip would be laid to rest, under the cypress trees of the graveyard in the stones. Leaderless, the shepherds had gone to Baas Gysbert to be given the day's work; and Hendrik Baadjies second shepherd, told Baas Gysbert that the police had taken Enoch Maarman at sunset, and now at dawn he had not yet returned, and that his wife was anxious. Would Baas Gysbert not please strike the telephone, not much only a little, not for long only a short time, to ask what had become of his father's head shepherd?

And Baas Gysbert replied in a voice trembling with passion, 'Do you not know it was my father who was killed?'

So Hendrik Baadjies touched his hat, and said, 'Pardon me, baas, that I asked.'

Then he went to stand with the other shepherds, a man shamed, a man shamed standing with other shamed men, who must teach their children to know for ever their station.

Fifteen hours. But she would not eat. Her neighbours brought food, but she would not. She could see the red foam at the corners of the mouth, and see the tremendous form and hear the tremendous voice that filled her house,

51

with anger, and with feigned politeness, and with contempt, and with cruel smiling. Because one was a shepherd, because one had no certitude of home or work or life or favour, because one's back had to be bent though one's soul would be upright, because one had to speak the smiling craven words under any injustice, because one had to bear as a brand this dark sun-warmed colour of the skin, as good surely as any other, because of these things, this mad policeman could strike down, and hold by the neck, and call a creeping yellow Hottentot bastard, a man who had never hurt another in his long gentle life, a man who like the great Christ was a lover of sheep and of little children, and had been a good husband and father except for those occasional outbursts that any sensible woman will pass over, outbursts of the imprisoned manhood that has got tired of the chains that keep it down on its knees. Yes this mad policeman could take off his hat mockingly in one's house, and ask a dozen questions that he, for all that he was as big as a mountain, would never have dared to ask a white person.

But the anger went from her suddenly, leaving her spent, leaving her again full of anxiety for the safety of her husband, and for the safety of her son who had chosen to come to Poort at this dangerous hour. Just as a person sits in the cold, and by keeping motionless enjoys some illusion of warmth, so she sat inwardly motionless, lest by some interior movement she would disturb the numbness of her mind, and feel the pain of her condition. However she was not allowed to remain so, for at eleven o'clock a message came from Hendrik Baadjies to say that it was certain that neither detective nor head shepherd was on the farm of Kroon. Then at noon a boy brought her a message that her brother Solomon Koopman had come with a taxi to the gate of the farm, and that she should come at once to him there, because he did not wish to come to her house. She tied a doek round her head, and as soon as she saw her brother, she cried to him, 'Are they safe?' When he looked mystified, she said, 'My man and my child,' and her brother told her it must have been Robbertse's joke, that her son was safe in Cape Town and had not been in Poort at all. He was glad to be able to tell her this piece of news, for his other news was terrible, that Enoch her husband was dead. He had always been a little afraid of his sister, who had brought up the family when their mother had died, so he did not know how to comfort her. But she wept only a little, like one who is used to such events, and must not grieve but must prepare for the next.

Then she said, 'How did he die?' So he told her the story that the police had told him of Enoch's death, how that the night was dark, and how they had gone searching down by the river, and how Enoch had slipped on one of the big stones there and had fallen on his head, and how they had not hesitated but had rushed him to Poort, but he had died in the car.

What can one say to a story like that? So they said nothing. He was ashamed to tell it, but he had to tell it so, because he had a butcher's licence in Poort, and he could not afford to doubt the police.

'This happened in the dark,' Sara said. 'Why do they let me know now?'

Alas, they could not give her her husband's body, it was buried already! Alas, she would know what it was like in the summer, how death began to smell because of the heat, that was why they had buried it! Alas, they wouldn't have done it had they only known who he was, and that his home was so near, at the well-known farm of Kroon!

Couldn't the body be lifted again, and be taken to Kroon, to be buried there in the hills where Enoch Maarman had worked so faithfully for nearly fifty years, tending the sheep of Big Baas Flip? Alas, no it couldn't be, for it is one thing to bury a man, and quite another thing to take him up again! To bury a man one only needs a doctor, and even that not always, but to take him up again you would have to go to Cape Town and get the permission of the Minister himself. And they do not permit that lightly, to disturb a man's bones when once he has been laid to rest in the earth.

Solomon Koopman would have gone away, with a smile on his lips, and cold hate in his heart. But she would not. For this surely was one thing that was her own, the body of the man she had lived with for so many years. She wanted the young white policeman behind the desk to show her the certificate of her husband's death, and she wanted to know by whose orders he had been buried, and who had hurried his body into the earth, so that she could tell for herself whether it was possible that such a person had not known that this was the body of Enoch Maarman, head shepherd of the farm of Kroon, who had that very night been in the company of Detective Robbertse.

She put these questions, through her brother Solomon Koopman, who had a butcher's licence, and framed the questions apologetically, because he knew that they implied that something was very wrong somewhere, that something was being hidden. But although he put the questions as nicely as possible, he could see that the policeman behind the desk was becoming impatient with this importunity, and was beginning to think that grief was no excuse for this cross-examination of authority. Other policeman came in too, and listened to the questions of this woman who would not go away, and one of them said to the young constable behind the desk, 'Show her the death certificate.'

There it was, 'Death due to sub-cranial bleeding.'

'He fell on his head,' explained the older policeman, 'and the blood inside finished him.'

'I ask to see Detective Robbertse,' she said.

The policemen smiled and looked at each other, not in any flagrant way, just knowingly.

'You can't see him,' said the older policeman. 'He went away on holiday this very morning.'

'Why does he go on holiday,' she asked, 'when he is working on this case?'

The policemen began to look at her impatiently. She was going too far, even though her husband was dead. Her own brother was growing restless, and he said to her, 'Sister, let us go.'

Her tears were coming now, made to flow by sorrow and anger. The policemen were uneasy, and drifted away, leaving only the young constable at the desk.

'What happened?' she asked. 'How did my husband die? Why is Detective Robbertse not here to answer my questions?'

The young policeman said to her angrily, 'We don't answer such questions here. If you want to ask such questions, get a lawyer.'

'Good,' she said. 'I shall get a lawyer.'

She and her brother turned to leave, but the older policeman was there at the door, polite and reasonable.

'Why isn't your sister sensible?' he asked Solomon Koopman. 'A lawyer will only stir up trouble between the police and the people.'

Koopman looked from the policeman to his sister, for he feared them both.

'Ask him,' Sara said to her brother, 'if it is not sensible to want to know about one's husband's death.'

'Tell her,' said the policeman to Koopman, 'that it was an accident.'

'He knows who I am,' Sara said. 'Why did he allow my husband to be buried here when he knew that he lived at Kroon.'

Her voice was rising, and to compensate for it, the policeman's voice grew lower and lower.

'I did not have him buried,' he said desperately. 'It was an order from a high person.'

Outside in the street, Koopman said to his sister miserably, 'Sister, I beg you, do not get a lawyer. For if you do, I shall lose the licence, and who will help you to keep your son at the university?'

Sara Maarman got back to her house as the sun was sinking over the hills of Kroon, twenty-four hours from the time that her husband had left with Detective Robbertse to look for the safe. She lit the lamp and sat down, too weary to think of food. While she sat there, Hendrik Baadjies knocked at the door and came in and brought her the sympathy of all the brown people on the farm of Kroon. Then he stood before her, twisting his hat in his hand almost as though she were a white woman. He brought a message from Baas Gysbert, who now needed a new shepherd and needed Enoch Maarman's house for him to live in. She would be given three days to pack all her possessions, and the loan of the cart and donkeys to take them and herself to Poort.

'Is three days enough?' asked Baadjies. 'For if it is not, I could ask for more.'

'Three days is enough,' she said.

When Baadjies had gone, she thought to herself, three days is three days too many, to go on living in this land of stone, three days before she could leave it all for the Cape, where her son lived, where people lived, so he told her, softer and sweeter lives.

Death of a Tsotsi

Abraham Moletisane was his name but no one ever called him anything but Spike. He was a true child of the city, gay, careless, plausible; but for all that, he was easy to manage and anxious to please. He was clean though flashy in his private dress. The khaki shirts and shorts of the reformatory were too drab for him, and he had a red scarf and yellow handkerchief which he arranged to peep out of his shirt pocket. He also had a pair of black and white shoes and a small but highly-coloured feather in his cap. Now the use of private clothes, except after the day's work, was forbidden; but he wore the red scarf on all occasions, saying, with an earnest expression that changed into an enigmatic smile if you looked too long at him, that his throat was sore. That was a great habit of his, to look away when you talked to him, and to smile at some unseen thing.

He passed through the first stages of the reformatory very successfully. He had two distinct sets of visitors, one his hard-working mother and his younger sister, and the other a group of flashy young men from the city. His mother and the young men never came together, and I think he arranged it so. While we did not welcome his second set of visitors, we did not forbid them so long as they behaved themselves; it was better for us to know about them than otherwise.

One day his mother and sister brought a friend Eliza-beth, who was a quiet and clean-looking person like themselves. Spike told me that his mother wished him to marry this girl, but that the girl was very independent, and refused to hear of it unless he reformed and gave up the company of the *tsotsis*.

'And what do you say, Spike?'

He would not look at me, but tilted his head up and surveyed the ceiling, smiling hard at it, and dropping his eyes but not his head to take an occasional glance at me. I did not know exactly what was in his mind, but it was clear to me that he was beginning to feel confidence in the reformatory.

'It doesn't help to say to her, just O.K., O.K.,' he said. 'She wants it done before everybody, as the Principal gives the first freedom.'

'What do you mean, before everybody?'

'Before my family and hers.'

'And are you willing?'

Spike smiled harder than ever at the ceiling, as though at some secret but delicious joy. Whether it was that he was savouring the delight of deciding his future, I do not know. Or whether he was savouring the delight of keeping guessing two whole families and the reformatory, I do not know either.

He was suddenly serious. 'If I promise her, I'll keep it,' he said. 'But I won't be forced.'

'No one's forcing you,' I said.

He lowered his head and looked at me, as though I did not understand the ways of women.

Although Spike was regarded as a weak character, he met all the temptations of increasing physical freedom very successfully. He went to the free hostels, and after some months there he received the privilege of special week-end leave to go home. He swaggered out, and he swaggered back, punctual to the minute. How he timed it I do not know, for he had no watch; but in all the months that he had privilege, he was never late.

It was just after he had received his first special leave that one of his city friends was sent to the reformatory also. The friend's name was Walter, and within a week of his arrival he and Spike had a fight, and both were sent to me. Walter alleged that Spike had hit him first, and Spike did not deny it.

'Why did you hit him, Spike?'

'He insulted me, meneer.'

'How?'

At length he came out with it.

'He said I was reformed.'

We could not help laughing at that, not much of course, for it was clear to me that Spike did not understand our laughter, and that he accepted it only because he knew we were well disposed towards him.

'If I said you were reformed, Spike,' I said, 'would you be insulted?'

'No, meneer.'

'Then why did he insult you?'

He thought that it was a difficult question. Then he said, 'He did not mean anything good, meneer. He meant I was back to being a child.'

'You are not,' I said. 'You are going forward to being a man.'

He was mollified by that, and I warned him not to fight again. He accepted my rebuke, but he said to me, 'This fellow is out to make trouble for me. He says I must go back to the *tsotsis* when I come out.'

I said to Walter, 'Did you say that?'

Walter was hurt to the depths and said, 'No, meneer.'

When they had gone I sent for de Villiers whose job it is to know every home in Johannesburg that has a boy at the reformatory. It was not an uncommon story, of a decent widow left with a son and daughter. She had managed to control the daughter, but not the son, and Spike had got in with a gang of *tsotsis*; as a result of one of their exploits he had found himself in court, but had not betrayed his friends. Then he had gone to the reformatory, which apart from anything it did itself, had enabled his mother to regain her hold on him, so that he had now decided to forsake the *tsotsis*, to get a job through de Villiers, and to marry the girl Elizabeth and live with her in his mother's house.

A week later Spike came to see me again.

'The Principal must forbid these friends of Walter to visit the reformatory,' he said.

'Why, Spike?'

'They are planning trouble for me, meneer.'

The boy was no longer smiling, but looked troubled, and I sat considering his request. I called in de Villiers, and we discussed it in Afrikaans, which Spike understood. But we were talking a rather high Afrikaans for him, and his eyes went from one face to the other, trying to follow what we said. If I forbade these boys to visit the reformatory, what help would that be to Spike? Would their resentment against him be any the less? Would they forget it because they did not see him? Might this not be a further cause for resentment against him? After all, one cannot remake the world; one can do all one can in a reformatory, but when the time comes, one has to take away one's hands. It was true that de Villiers would look after him, but such supervision had its defined limits. As I looked at the boy's troubled face, I also was full of trouble for him; for he had of his choice bound himself with chains, and now, when he wanted of his choice to put them off, he found it was not so easy to do. He looked at us intently, and I could see that he felt excluded, and wished to be brought in again.

'Did you understand what we said, Spike?'

'Not everything, meneer.'

'I am worried about one thing,' I said. 'Which is better for you, to forbid these boys, or not to forbid them?'

'To forbid them,' he said.

'They might say,' I said, ' "Now he'll pay for this." '

'The Principal does not understand,' he said. 'My time is almost finished at the reformatory. I don't want trouble before I leave.'

'I'm not worried about trouble here,' I said. 'I'm worried about trouble outside.'

He looked at me anxiously, as though I had not fully grasped the matter.

'I'm not worried about here,' I said with asperity. 'I can look after you here. If someone tried to make trouble, do you think I can't find the truth?'

He did not wish to doubt my ability, but he remained anxious.

'You still want me to forbid them?' I asked.

'Yes, meneer.'

'Mr de Villiers,' I said, 'find out all you can about these boys. Then let me know.'

'And then,' I said to Spike, 'I'll talk to you about forbidding them.'

'They're a tough lot,' de Villiers told me later. 'No parental control. In fact they have left home and are living with George, the head of the gang. George's mother is quite without hope for her son, but she's old now and depends on him. He gives her money, and she sees nothing, hears nothing, says nothing. She cooks for them.'

'And they won't allow Spike to leave the gang?' I asked.

'I couldn't prove that, but it's a funny business. The reason why they don't want to let Spike go is because he has the brains and the courage. He makes the plans and they all obey him on the job. But off the job he's nobody. Off the job they all listen to George.'

'Did you see George?'

'I saw George,' he said, 'and I reckon he's a bad fellow. He's morose and sullen, and physically bigger than Spike.'

'If you got in his way,' he added emphatically, 'he'd wipe you out – like that.'

We both sat there rather gloomy about Spike's future.

'Spike's the best of the lot,' he said. 'It's tragic that he ever got in with them. Now that he wants to get out . . . well . . .'

He left his sentence unfinished.

'Let's see him,' I said.

'We've seen these friends of Walter's,' I said to Spike, 'and we don't like them very much. But whether it will help to forbid their visits, I truly do not know. But I am willing to do what you say.'

'The Principal must forbid them,' he said at once.

So I forbade them. They listened to me in silence, neither humble nor insolent, nor affronted nor surprised; they put up no pleas or protests. George said, 'Good, sir,' and one by one they followed him out.

When a boy finally leaves the reformatory, he is usually

elated, and does not hide his high spirits. He comes to the office for a final conversation, and goes off like one who has brought off an extraordinary coup. But Spike was subdued.

'Spike,' I said privately, with only de Villiers there, 'are you afraid?'

He looked down at the floor and said, 'I'm not afraid,' as though his fear were private also, and would neither be lessened nor made greater by confession.

He was duly married and de Villiers and I made him a present of a watch so that he could always be on time for his work. He had a good job in a factory in Industria, and worked magnificently; he saved money, and spent surprisingly little on clothes. But he had none of his old gaiety and attractive carelessness. He came home promptly, and once home, never stirred out.

It was summer when he was released, and with the approach of winter he asked if de Villiers would not see the manager of the factory, and arrange for him to leave half an hour earlier, so that he could reach his home before dark. But the manager said it was impossible, as Spike was on the kind of job that would come to a standstill if one man left earlier. De Villiers waited for him after work, and he could see that the boy was profoundly depressed.

'Have they said anything to you?' de Villiers asked him.

The boy would not answer for a long time, and at last he said with a finality that was meant to stop further discussion, 'They'll get me.' He was devoid of hope, and did not wish to talk about it, like a man who has a great pain and does not wish to discuss it, but prefers to suffer it alone and silent. This hopelessness had affected his wife and mother and sister, so that all of them sat darkly and heavily. And de Villiers noted that there were new bars on every door and window. So he left darkly and heavily too, and Spike went with him to the little gate.

And Spike asked him, 'Can I carry a knife?'

It was a hard question and the difficulty of it angered de Villiers, so that he said harshly, 'How can I say that you can carry a knife?'

'You,' said Spike, 'my mother, my sister, Elizabeth.' He looked at de Villiers.

'I obey you all,' he said, and went back into the house.

So still more darkly and heavily de Villiers went back to the reformatory and, sitting in my office, communicated his mood to me. We decided that he would visit Spike more often than he visited any other boy. This he did, and he even went to the length of calling frequently at the factory at five o'clock, and taking Spike home. He tried to cheer and encourage the boy, but the dark heavy mood could not be shifted.

One day Spike said to him, 'I tell you, sir, you all did your best for me.'

The next day he was stabbed to death just by the little gate.

In spite of my inside knowledge, Spike's death so shocked me that I could do no work. I sat in my office, hopeless and defeated. Then I sent for the boy Walter.

'I sent for you,' I said, 'to tell you that Spike is dead.'

He had no answer to make. Nothing showed in his face to tell whether he cared whether Spike were alive or dead. He stood there impassively, obedient and respectful, ready to go or ready to stand there for ever.

'He's dead,' I said angrily. 'He was killed. Don't you care?'

'I care,' he said.

He would have cared very deeply, had I pressed him. He surveyed me unwinkingly, ready to comply with my slightest request. Between him and me there was an un-bridgeable chasm; so far as I know there was nothing in the world, not one hurt or grievance or jest or sorrow, that could have stirred us both together.

Therefore I let him go.

De Villiers and I went to the funeral, and spoke words of sympathy to Spike's mother and wife and sister. But the words fell like dead things to the ground, for something deeper than sorrow was there. We were all of us, white and black, rich and poor, learned and untutored, bowed down by a knowledge that we lived in the shadow of a great danger, and were powerless against it. It was no place for a white person to pose in any mantle of power or authority; for this death gave the lie to both of them.

And this death would go on too, for nothing less than the reform of a society would bring it to an end. It was the menace of the socially frustrated, strangers to mercy, striking like adders for the dark reasons of ancient minds at any who crossed their paths.

The Worst Thing of His Life

You never get used to absconding. I remember once we went for sixty-one days without an absconder; there were six hundred boys in the reformatory, and nearly half of them could have walked away at any time. Day after day went past of peace unbroken except for trifling offences, and you couldn't help being proud of it, though you kept your pride secret so that no hand out of the sky could strike you down for presumption. Then on the sixty-second day a boy ran away, and we were as downcast as though the sixty-one days had never happened. Somehow you never got used to it.

A time of heavy absconding was a trial of the soul. You felt as though the whole institution were cracking and breaking; you felt you were inefficient, a bungler, a theorist who had theories but no knowledge of human nature; you felt judged even by your own staff and your own boys. And you feared too, although you didn't talk about it, that some newspaper would get hold of it, and print in some careless corner the words that would bring your career to an end, and kill the faith in your heart that your way was the right way, and make you nothing in the eyes of the world and your wife and children. For the Principal of a great institution has almost divine powers, and is admired by his friends and family.

Of course if your reformatory is what is called 'closed', then you can put the blame for absconding on to the perversity of human nature; you can join the public heartily when it curses your absconders. But when your reformatory is half 'open', and when you yourself made it so, you can't blame anyone but yourself. Of course if a staff member has been negligent, you can purge yourself by rebuking him beyond reason; but then you are ashamed, and you remember how he stood by you during some trouble, so you go and apologize to him.

Half of your absconders are probably 'free' boys. Their absconding worries you more than the others, because they promised you certain things when you gave them their freedom. Some abscond and stay away; some abscond, and after dark return secretly and sheepishly to your house; one got to Durban, four hundred miles away, and there gave himself up to the police.

If a 'free' absconder commits some serious offence while he is at large, that is hard to bear, because you feel directly responsible. It is sometimes difficult to decide whether to make a boy 'free', because although his conduct is exemplary, he perhaps committed some violent offence before he came to you. You are torn in two, because you wish by this encouragement to confirm him in his resolution to be law-abiding, yet you are afraid that he may endanger you and your career by some violent act.

When such a boy does abscond, and shortly afterwards some unknown person commits such an act, your mind is full of anxiety, and you fear the worst. You sleep badly at night, and dread the ringing of the telephone. Sometimes hundreds of police are called out after such an offence, and you are tormented by the thought that perhaps you are responsible for all this expenditure of time and effort, and for some innocent person's suffering.

After my first five years the reformatory began to settle down after having been disturbed by these new experiments. As far as absconding was concerned, the new freedom was working as well as the old strict watchfulness. But the new freedom liberated not only boys, but new energies and strengths from the unprofitable task of watching; one could now turn to the real work of education. Yet, though year succeeded year in comparative tranquillity, the old fear was never quite banished; the ring of the telephone, especially in the sleeping hours, was enough to set the heart beating.

One night after my wife and I had gone to bed, I was awakened by the sound of footsteps on the gravel outside the window, followed by a respectful knock.

'Who's there?' I asked.

'It's me, sir, Jonkers,' a voice said in Afrikaans.

If I could be called the colonel of the reformatory, then Jonkers was the adjutant, the chief executive officer. It was a tough job with a heavy responsibility, and a day that began at six in the morning and ended at six at night, with the likelihood of being called out at any time thereafter. He was a simple man of no great education, but with a loyalty and devotion that no man ever surpassed; he had stood by me in all kinds of crises and troubles, and in his simple way understood what I was doing and believed in it.

His voice was low and trembling, so I made mine matter-of-fact and firm, and said, 'What's the matter?'

'There's great trouble,' he said.

He had never said that to me before, and I thought with pain, now it has come, just when we thought all danger was past.

'Go round to the front door,' I said.

I put on my dressing-gown and slippers, and said to my wife, 'It's some trouble.'

When I let Jonkers in, I was shocked by his appearance.

The big man would not look at me, but with exaggerated politeness edged himself in at the door, and did not sit down till I had asked him to.

I sat down too, and said to him with fear in my heart, 'What's the trouble?'

He made no answer, but sat there trying to control himself and I sat watching him, both of us full of misery. But I put on a brave front to him, and waited quietly for him to speak, as though I had great resources on which to draw when the need would arise. Still he did not speak, and I said to him, 'Take your time.'

He said, with a kind of brave gratitude, 'Dankie, meneer.' He sat there in front of me, humble and shaken, and did not know he was in fact tormenting me: he did not know he was in fact standing over me, with an axe or a club, and that I was crying out to him, 'For God's sake, strike me, but don't torment me.'

'You're upset,' I said.

Again he gave me the look of humble thanks. He was thanking me, the Principal with great powers, for noticing his suffering, as though it were kind of me, as though I were not sitting there consumed with desperate anxiety about myself and my work.

'I'm finished,' he said.

I did not know what he meant. He might have meant he was exhausted, all resources gone. Or he might have meant, and that would have been in character with him, that his career was finished. Because he would take the blame, I knew that. He would fear my wrath, but it would not occur to him that if he was finished, I would be finished too.

'It's the worst thing of my life,' he said.

'What is?'

'Sir, I can't bring myself to tell you,' he said. Then he said, 'I've told the Principal some bad news in my life, but I don't know how to tell him this.'

Then a car drew up outside the house, and doors banged, and men came running. And I thought, let them all come, and went out on to the stoep to meet them.

Fichardt said to me, 'Is Mr Jonkers here?'

'He's here,' I said.

'Thank God,' he said in a low voice. 'I was afraid he might do something desperate.'

And I said, also in a low voice, 'What's the trouble?' And I braced myself for the worst.

'It's his son, sir. He's just had a message to say his son's been arrested.'

So the great fear rolled off my heart, there on the stoep. The relief was so great that my whole self had to experience it, and for a moment, no, for some moments, I had no thought to spare for Jonkers and his son. Then I said quietly, 'What for?'

'I don't know, sir.'

Fichardt and I went into the house, where Jonkers was sitting with his head in his hands.

'He's worried about the boy, sir,' said Fichardt. Then he added with meaning, 'He's worried about his job too.'

I went to Jonkers.

'Are you worried about the job?' I said.

He nodded and wept openly, a public servant in danger, and a father in disgrace.

'If they take away your job,' I said, 'they can take away mine too.'

The big man did not, could not, look at me, but I heard him saying in a broken voice, 'Dankie, meneer: dankie meneer.'

'I couldn't run this place without you,' I said.

Even in the midst of his weeping he could not hide his pride. Then he said to me, 'I'm ashamed. I'm an elder in the church. There's never been a thing like this in our family.'

I was full of confidence and strength.

'We'll go to the police,' I said. 'It's some boy's trick. Perhaps he was showing off in a car. I'll go and get dressed.'

Jonkers looked at me with gratitude. I could see that he was grateful to be going to the police with the Principal. Fichardt went back to the car, and I went to get dressed.

'Trouble?' asked my wife.

'Trouble,' I said. 'But not the reformatory.'

'Good,' she said, and went to sleep.

When I got back to Jonkers, he was standing up waiting for me.

'Meneer,' he said.

'Yes.'

'I hope I didn't frighten you,' he said. 'You might have thought it was trouble at the reformatory.'

'Of course not,' I said, 'of course not.'

'I told my wife,' he said, 'I'm down as far as a man can go, but if I go to the Principal he'll lift me up.'

'That's good,' I said. 'Let's go.'

The Waste Land

The moment that the bus moved on he knew he was in danger, for by the lights of it he saw the figures of the young men waiting under the tree. That was the thing feared by all, to be waited for by the young men. It was a thing he had talked about, now he was to see it for himself.

It was too late to run after the bus; it went down the dark street like an island of safety in a sea of perils. Though he had known of his danger only for a second, his mouth was already dry, his heart was pounding in his breast, something within him was crying out in protest against the coming event.

His wages were in his purse, he could feel them weighing heavily against his thigh. That was what they wanted from him. Nothing counted against that. His wife could be made a widow, his children made fatherless, nothing counted against that. Mercy was the unknown word.

While he stood there irresolute he heard the young men walking towards him, not only from the side where he had seen them, but from the other also. They did not speak, their intention was unspeakable. The sound of their feet came on the wind to him. The place was well chosen, for behind him was the high wall of the convent, and the barred door that would not open before a man was dead. On the other side of the road was the waste land, full of wire and iron and the bodies of old cars. It was his only hope, and he moved towards it; as he did so he knew from the whistle that the young men were there too.

His fear was great and instant, and the smell of it went from his body to his nostrils. At that very moment one of them spoke, giving directions. So trapped was he that he was filled suddenly with strength and anger, and he ran towards the waste land swinging his heavy stick. In the darkness a form loomed up at him, and he swung the stick at it, and heard it give a cry of pain. Then he plunged blindly into the wilderness of wire and iron and the bodies of old cars.

Something caught him by the leg, and he brought his stick crashing down on it, but it was no man, only some knife-edged piece of iron. He was sobbing and out of breath, but he pushed on into the waste, while behind him they pushed on also, knocking against the old iron bodies and kicking against tins and buckets. He fell into some grotesque shape of wire; it was barbed and tore at his clothes and flesh. Then it held him, so that it seemed to him that death must be near, and having no other hope, he cried out, 'Help me, help me!' in what should have been a great voice but was voiceless and gasping. He tore at the wire, and it tore at him too, ripping his face and his hands.

Then suddenly he was free. He saw the bus returning, and he cried out again in the great voiceless voice, 'Help me, help me!' Against the lights of it he could plainly see the form of one of the young men. Death was near him, and for a moment he was filled with the injustice of life, that could end thus for one who had always been hard-working and law-abiding. He lifted the heavy stick and brought it down on the head of his pursuer, so that the man crumpled to the ground, moaning and groaning as though life had been unjust to him also.

Then he turned and began to run again, but ran first

into the side of an old lorry which sent him reeling. He lay there for a moment expecting the blow that would end him, but even then his wits came back to him, and he turned over twice and was under the lorry. His very entrails seemed to be coming into his mouth, and his lips could taste sweat and blood. His heart was like a wild thing in his breast, and seemed to lift his whole body each time that it beat. He tried to calm it down, thinking it might be heard, and tried to control the noise of his gasping breath, but he could not do either of these things.

Then suddenly against the dark sky he saw two of the young men. He thought they must hear him; but they themselves were gasping like drowned men, and their speech came by fits and starts.

Then one of them said, 'Do you hear?'

They were silent except for their gasping, listening. And he listened also, but could hear nothing but his own exhausted heart.

'I heard a man . . . running . . . on the road,' said one. 'He's got away . . . let's go.'

Then some more of the young men came up, gasping and cursing the man who had got away.

'Freddy,' said one, 'your father's got away.'

But there was no reply.

'Where's Freddy?' one asked.

One said, 'Quiet!' Then he called in a loud voice, 'Freddy.'

But still there was no reply.

'Let's go,' he said.

They moved off slowly and carefully, then one of them stopped.

'We are saved,' he said. 'Here is the man.'

He knelt down on the ground, and then fell to cursing.

'There's no money here,' he said.

One of them lit a match, and in the small light of it the man under the lorry saw him fall back.

'It's Freddy,' one said. 'He's dead.'

Then the one who had said 'Quiet' spoke again.

'Lift him up,' he said. 'Put him under the lorry.'

The man under the lorry heard them struggling with the body of the dead young man, and he turned once, twice, deeper into his hiding-place. The young men lifted the body and swung it under the lorry so that it touched him. Then he heard them moving away, not speaking, slowly and quietly, making an occasional sound against some obstruction in the waste.

He turned on his side, so that he would not need to touch the body of the young man. He buried his face in his arms, and said to himself in the idiom of his own language, 'People, arise! The world is dead.' Then he arose himself, and went heavily out of the waste land.

A Drink in the Passage

In the year 1960 the Union of South Africa celebrated its Golden Jubilee, and there was a nation-wide sensation when the one-thousand-pound prize for the finest piece of sculpture was won by a black man, Edward Simelane. His work, 'African Mother and Child', not only excited the admiration, but touched the conscience or heart or whatever it is, of white South Africa, and was likely to make him famous in other countries.

It was by an oversight that his work was accepted, for it was the policy of the Government that all the celebrations and competitions should be strictly segregated. The committee of the sculpture section received a private reprimand for having been so careless as to omit the words 'for whites only' from the conditions, but was told, by a very high personage it is said, that if Simelane's work was indisputably the best, it should receive the award. The committee then decided that this prize must be given along with the others, at the public ceremony which would bring this particular part of the celebrations to a close.

For this decision it received a surprising amount of support from the white public, but in certain powerful quarters there was an outcry against any departure from the 'traditional policies' of the country, and a threat that many white prize-winners would renounce their prizes. However, a crisis was averted, because the sculptor was 'unfortunately unable to attend the ceremony'.

'I wasn't feeling up to it,' Simelane said mischievously to me. 'My parents, and my wife's parents, and our priest, decided that I wasn't feeling up to it. And finally I decided so too. Of course Majosi and Sola and the others wanted me to go and get my prize personally, but I said, "Boys, I'm a sculptor, not a demonstrator."'

'This cognac is wonderful,' he said, 'especially in these big glasses. It's the first time I've had such a glass. It's also the first time I've drunk a brandy so slowly. In Orlando you develop a throat of iron, and you just put back your head and pour it down, in case the police should arrive.'

He said to me, 'This is the second cognac I've had in my life. Would you like to hear the story of how I had my first?'

You know the Alabaster Bookshop in Von Brandis Street? Well, after the competition they asked me if they could exhibit my 'African Mother and Child'. They gave a whole window to it, with a white velvet backdrop, if there is anything called white velvet, and some complimentary words, *Black man conquers white world.*

Well somehow I could never go and look in that window. On my way from the station to the Herald office, I sometimes went past there, and I felt good when I saw all the people standing there, but I would only squint at it out of the corner of my eye.

Then one night I was working late at the Herald, and when I came out there was hardly anyone in the streets, so I thought I'd go and see the window, and indulge certain pleasurable human feelings. I must have got a little lost in the contemplation of my own genius, because suddenly there was a young white man standing next to me.

He said to me, 'What do you think of that, mate?' And you know, one doesn't get called 'mate' every day.

'I'm looking at it,' I said.

'I live near here,' he said, 'and I come and look at it nearly every night. You know it's by one of your own boys, don't you? See, Edward Simelane.'

'Yes, I know.'

'It's beautiful,' he said. 'Look at that mother's head. She's loving that child, but she's somehow watching too. Do you see that? Like someone guarding. She knows it won't be an easy life.'

He cocked his head on one side, to see the thing better.

'He got a thousand pounds for it,' he said.

'That's a lot of money for one of your boys. But good luck to him. You don't get much luck, do you?'

Then he said confidentially, 'Mate, would you like a drink?'

Well honestly I didn't feel like a drink at that time of night, with a white stranger and all, and me still with a train to catch to Orlando.

'You know we black people must be out of the city by eleven,' I said.

'It won't take long. My flat's just round the corner. Do you speak Afrikaans?'

'Since I was a child,' I said in Afrikaans.

'We'll speak Afrikaans then. My English isn't too wonderful. I'm van Rensburg. And you?'

I couldn't have told him my name. I said I was Vakalisa, living in Orlando.

'Vakalisa, eh? I haven't heard that name before.'

By this time he had started off, and I was following, but not willingly. That's my trouble, as you'll soon see. I can't break off an encounter. We didn't exactly walk abreast, but he didn't exactly walk in front of me. He didn't look constrained. He wasn't looking round to see if anyone might be watching.

He said to me, 'Do you know what I wanted to do?'

'No,' I said.

'I wanted a bookshop, like that one there. I always wanted that, ever since I can remember. When I was small, I had a little shop of my own.' He laughed at himself. 'Some were real books, of course, but some of them I wrote myself. But I had bad luck. My parents died before I could finish school.'

Then he said to me, 'Are you educated?'

I said unwillingly, 'Yes.' Then I thought to myself, how stupid, for leaving the question open.

And sure enough he asked, 'Far?'

And again unwillingly, I said, 'Far.'

He took a big leap and said, 'Degree?'

'Yes.'

'Literature?'

'Yes.'

He expelled his breath, and gave a long 'Ah'. We had reached his building, Majorca Mansions, not one of those luxurious places. I was glad to see that the entrance lobby was deserted. I wasn't at my ease. I don't feel at my ease in such places, not unless I am protected by friends, and this man was a stranger. The lift was at ground level, marked 'Whites only. Slegs vir Blankes.' Van Rensburg opened the door and waved me in. Was he constrained? To this day I don't know. While I was waiting for him to press the button, so that we could get moving and away from that ground floor, he stood with his finger suspended over it, and looked at me with a kind of honest, unselfish envy.

'You were lucky,' he said. 'Literature, that's what I wanted to do.'

He shook his head and pressed the button, and he didn't

speak again until we stopped high up. But before we got out he said suddenly, 'If I had had a bookshop, I'd have given that boy a window too.'

We got out and walked along one of those polished concrete passageways, I suppose you could call it a stoep if it weren't so high up; let's call it a passage. On the one side was a wall, and plenty of fresh air, and far down below, Von Brandis Street. On the other side were the doors, impersonal doors; you could hear radios and people talking, but there wasn't a soul in sight. I wouldn't like living so high; we Africans like being close to the earth. Van Rensburg stopped at one of the doors, and said to me, 'I won't be a minute.' Then he went in, leaving the door open, and inside I could hear voices. I thought to myself, he's telling them who's here. Then after a minute or so, he came back to the door, holding two glasses of red wine. He was warm and smiling.

'Sorry there's no brandy,' he said. 'Only wine. Here's happiness.'

Now I certainly had not expected that I would have my drink in the passage. I wasn't only feeling what you may be thinking. I was thinking that one of the impersonal doors might open at any moment, and someone might see me in a 'white' building, and see me and van Rensburg breaking the liquor laws of the country. Anger could have saved me from the whole embarrassing situation, but you know I can't easily be angry. Even if I could have been, I might have found it hard to be angry with this particular man. But I wanted to get away from there, and I couldn't. My mother used to say to me, when I had said something anti-white, 'Son, don't talk like that, talk as you are.' She would have understood at once why I took a drink from a man who gave it to me in the passage.

Van Rensburg said to me, 'Don't you know this fellow Simelane?'

'I've heard of him,' I said.

'I'd like to meet him,' he said. 'I'd like to talk to him.' He added in explanation, 'You know, talk out my heart to him.'

A woman of about fifty years of age came from the room beyond, bringing a plate of biscuits. She smiled and bowed to me. I took one of the biscuits, but not for all the money in the world could I have said to her 'Dankie, my nooi,' or that disgusting 'Dankie, missus,' nor did I want to speak to her in English because her language was Afrikaans, so I took the risk of it and used the word '*mevrou*' for the politeness of which some Afrikaners would knock a black man down, and I said, in high Afrikaans, with a smile and a bow too, 'Ek is u dankbaar, mevrou.'

But nobody knocked me down. The woman smiled and bowed, and van Rensburg, in a strained voice that suddenly came out of nowhere, said, 'Our land is beautiful. But it breaks my heart.'

The woman put her hand on his arm, and said, 'Jannie, Jannie.'

Then another woman and a man, all about the same age, came up and stood behind van Rensburg.

'He's a B.A.,' van Rensburg told them. 'What do you think of that?'

The first woman smiled and bowed to me again, and van Rensburg said, as though it were a matter for grief, 'I wanted to give him brandy, but there's only wine.'

The second woman said, 'I remember, Jannie. Come with me.'

She went back into the room, and he followed her. The

first woman said to me, 'Jannie's a good man. Strange, but good.'

And I thought the whole thing was mad, and getting beyond me, with me a black stranger being shown a testimonial for the son of the house, with these white strangers standing and looking at me in the passage, as though they wanted for God's sake to touch me somewhere and didn't know how, but I saw the earnestness of the woman who had smiled and bowed to me, and I said to her, 'I can see that, mevrou.'

'He goes down every night to look at the statue,' she said. 'He says only God could make something so beautiful, therefore God must be in the man who made it, and he wants to meet him and talk out his heart to him.'

She looked back at the room, and then she dropped her voice a little, and said to me, 'Can't you see, it's somehow because it's a black woman and a black child?'

And I said to her, 'I can see that, mevrou.'

She turned to the man and said of me, 'He's a good boy.'

Then the other woman returned with van Rensburg, and van Rensburg had a bottle of brandy. He was smiling and pleased, and he said to me, 'This isn't ordinary brandy, it's French.'

He showed me the bottle, and I, wanting to get the hell out of that place, looked at it and saw it was cognac. He turned to the man and said, 'Uncle, you remember? When you were ill? The doctor said you must have good brandy. And the man at the bottle-store said this was the best brandy in the world.'

'I must go,' I said. 'I must catch that train.'

'I'll take you to the station,' he said. 'Don't you worry about that.'

He poured me a drink and one for himself.

'Uncle,' he said, 'what about one for yourself?'

The older man said, 'I don't mind if I do,' and he went inside to get himself a glass.

Van Rensburg said, 'Happiness,' and lifted his glass to me. It was good brandy, the best I've ever tasted. But I wanted to get the hell out of there. I stood in the passage and drank van Rensburg's brandy. Then Uncle came back with his glass, and van Rensburg poured him a brandy, and Uncle raised his glass to me too. All of us were full of goodwill, but I was waiting for the opening of one of the impersonal doors. Perhaps they were too, I don't know. Perhaps when you want so badly to touch someone you don't care. I was drinking my brandy almost as fast as I would have drunk it in Orlando.

'I must go,' I said.

Van Rensburg said, 'I'll take you to the station.' He finished his brandy, and I finished mine too. We handed the glasses to Uncle, who said to me, 'Good night, my boy.' The first woman said, 'May God bless you,' and the other woman bowed and smiled. Then van Rensburg and I went down in the lift to the basement, and got into his car.

'I told you I'd take you to the station,' he said. 'I'd take you home, but I'm frightened of Orlando at night.'

We drove up Eloff Street, and he said, 'Did you know what I meant?' I knew that he wanted an answer to something, and I wanted to answer him, but I couldn't, because I didn't know what that something was. He couldn't be talking about being frightened of Orlando at night, because what more could one mean than just that?

'By what?' I asked.

'You know,' he said, 'about our land being beautiful?'

Yes, I knew what he meant, and I knew that for God's sake he wanted to touch me too and he couldn't; for his eyes had been blinded by years in the dark. And I thought it was a pity, for if men never touch each other, they'll hurt each other one day. And it was a pity he was blind, and couldn't touch me, for black men don't touch white men any more; only by accident, when they make something like 'Mother and Child'.

He said to me, 'What are you thinking?'

I said, 'Many things,' and my inarticulateness distressed me, for I knew he wanted something from me. I felt him fall back, angry, hurt, despairing, I didn't know. He stopped at the main entrance to the station, but I didn't tell him I couldn't go in there. I got out and said to him, 'Thank you for the sociable evening.'

'They liked having you,' he said. 'Did you see that they did?'

I said, 'Yes, I saw that they did.'

He sat slumped in his seat, like a man with a burden of incomprehensible, insoluble grief. I wanted to touch him, but I was thinking about the train. He said good night, and I said it too. We each saluted the other. What he was thinking, God knows, but I was thinking he was like a man trying to run a race in iron shoes, and not understanding why he cannot move.

When I got back to Orlando, I told my wife the story, and she wept.

Sponono

This very day I received a letter from Sponono, full of reproaches. He asks why I have not answered his previous letter. He writes to me, 'Are you then like other people, who, when a man has done wrong, treat him badly? I have always looked upon you as trustworthy, but now I am ashamed in front of my friends.' He asks, 'Why have you turned? You were always a man of your word, but now you are changed.' He concludes that this turning of mine is 'wonderful'.

I feel I must put up some kind of defence against this indictment which questions qualities of my character of whose existence I have been moderately certain. Whether his friends will ever read it, and refrain from harsh judgements on that account, is very improbable. But it will at least give me the opportunity of describing an engaging rascal, who expected my conduct towards him to surpass in superhuman degree his conduct towards me. How did he ever formulate such noble ideals of behaviour? That I do not know, for he certainly did not practise them. Nevertheless he knew of them, and while he considered himself too frail to practise them, he expected me to do so, and never failed to reproach me when I fell short of them. Yet on one occasion he did practise them, under the most unlikely circumstances, with an ease and grace that would have done credit to a saint.

Sponono was a Xhosa boy, about sixteen years old when he first came to the reformatory. My first intimate encounter with him was certainly extraordinary. He had asked to see the Principal, on urgent private business, and accordingly he was brought to me by the Chief Supervisor, Mr van Dyk.

'Well, Sponono,' I said, 'I hear you want to see me.'

'Yes, meneer,' he said.

'What is your trouble?' I asked.

'I have no trouble,' he said. 'I have come to see you about the trouble of Johannes Mofoking.'

'Are you a friend of his?' I asked.

'I am not a friend of his,' he said, 'but I have heard about his case, and it is about his case that I wish to speak with you.'

By this time Mr van Dyk was looking somewhat uncomfortable, because it was a rule that any boy wishing to see me must first state his business clearly to the Chief Supervisor, unless he could claim that the matter was confidential and private. But I told Mr van Dyk to put himself at ease, and I said to Sponono, 'What about Johannes Mofoking?'

'We all know,' he said, 'that Johannes Mofoking ran away from the reformatory, and that when he was captured and sent back here, he was in possession of a gold watch.'

'That is so,' I said.

'Some of us think,' said Sponono, 'that you are being too severe. Johannes admitted that he had stolen the watch, and he did not lie about it. This makes us think that he is not a bad fellow, and he himself does not wish to go to prison, but says he is willing to do some extra time in the reformatory to atone for what he has done.'

'That is very good of him,' I said.

'Sir,' said Mr van Dyk, 'I had no idea . . .'

'Do not trouble yourself,' I said. 'Sponono, you must know that I cannot conceal the theft of this watch from the police. Furthermore . . .'

'Meneer,' he said, 'we do not . . .'

'Excuse me, sir,' said Mr van Dyk. 'Sponono, you must not interrupt the Principal when he is speaking. It is not proper.'

'I ask pardon,' said Sponono, humbly, 'I did not mean to interrupt the Principal.'

'Go on,' I said.

'Meneer,' said Sponono, 'we do not ask you to conceal the theft of the watch from the police.'

'That is good of you,' I said.

'Meneer,' he said, ignoring my own interruptions, 'we are satisfied that he should go to court. All we ask is that you should ask the court to send him back to the reformatory. Otherwise, he may grow into a bad fellow, and we are sure you do not wish this to happen.'

'He is getting old,' I said. 'He is nearly twenty.'

'I admit he is nearly twenty,' said Sponono. 'But he is not a bad fellow. But if he goes to prison, I fear he will become hard.'

'The reformatory is very full,' I said. 'We have more than six hundred boys now, and the reformatory is built for only four hundred.'

'My room is not full,' said Sponono. 'He can sleep there.'

'That is very good of you,' I said. It was the third time I had made such a remark, but of the sarcasm he took as little notice as before.

'I thought it would be wrong to send Johannes to prison,' he said. 'I told a lie to the Chief Supervisor when I said I had private business, because I knew that if I had told him my real business, he would not have allowed me to see you.'

'Do you not think it wrong to tell a lie?' I asked.

'Not to save a person,' he said.

'Mr van Dyk,' I said, 'bring Johannes to me.'

Johannes was brought, and I said to him, 'Johannes, I understand that you are ready to go to court, and to plead guilty to stealing this watch, but that you wish to be sent back to the reformatory.'

'That is true, meneer.'

'But,' I said, 'you are nearly twenty, and if you have not yet learned to stop stealing, what good will it do to teach you all over again?'

'I am learning,' he said, 'but not yet enough. If I come back here, I shall learn completely. But if I go to prison, I shall learn to steal more than before.'

'In that case,' I said, 'I shall ask the court to send you back here.'

'Thank you, meneer,' he said.

'Don't thank me,' I said. 'Thank Sponono. He was the one who spoke for you.'

Johannes turned to Sponono. 'Thank you,' he said.

'Do not thank me,' said Sponono. 'Thank the Principal. Without him I could have done nothing.'

It was about a month later that Sponono asked to see me again.

'Is it more private business?' I asked Mr van Dyk.

Mr van Dyk smiled at me in a reproachful manner.

'Sponono wishes to work in your garden,' he said.

'William is already working in my garden,' I said.

'Your garden is not properly cared for,' said Sponono. 'William is a good fellow, but he does not fully understand the work of a garden.'

'What must I say to William?' I asked. 'Must I say to him that you do not approve of his work in the garden, and that you have appointed yourself in his place?'

'I do not say that,' said Sponono. 'Let me work under him until he is discharged. That will be very soon.'

'How do you know that?' I asked.

'He told me,' he said.

'Did you arrange it between you?' I asked. And when he did not answer I asked again, 'Shall I tell William that he does not understand the work of a garden?'

'That would only make trouble,' he said. 'Let me work under him.'

I must report that Sponono did not prove a good subordinate. William would come and complain to me that Sponono would not do what he was told to do. Sponono would come and complain to me that William was inefficient, lazy, and dishonest. I was compelled to divide the garden into two portions, and I must admit that Sponono proved an excellent gardener. But between him and William there was endless friction, until William was discharged, and Sponono took command. Then Sponono began to complain about the new assistant, a very meek fellow named George. But things went reasonably smoothly until Christmas Day.

Christmas Day was a big day at the reformatory, with special meals, a sports meeting with prizes, and gifts of sweets for the younger and tobacco for the older boys. I returned home at sunset after a hot and tiring day, looking forward to our own family Christmas and pleasant relaxation. But I had hardly sat down with our guests when the telephone recalled me to the office, where a harassed Mr van Dyk introduced me to a distraught Mr Anderson, who told me the following disturbing tale.

Mr Anderson and his wife had packed a picnic basket that morning, and had found a shady spot on the eastern portion of the reformatory farm, where they had enjoyed a good lunch of Christmas fare and some iced beer, after which they had lain down in the grass for a pleasant siesta. But their siesta was to prove anything but pleasant. They had been wakened rudely by a boy in clothes identical with the reformatory uniform, a khaki shirt and khaki shorts. This boy had menaced them with a large stone and had snatched up Mrs Anderson's hand-bag from the grass, and made off into the bushes. In the hand-bag was sixty pounds, in twelve five-pound notes, a whole month's earnings, and the distress of husband and wife was painful to see.

'I know I should have had permission,' said Mr Anderson, 'but there was no one to be seen, and it was an ideal spot for a picnic. At least, we thought it was until this terrible thing happened.'

'If it was one of our boys, Mr Anderson,' I said, 'I hope we shall be able to find him. Most of the boys were at the sports, and we naturally have to know precisely where each one is on such an occasion. Did you find everything correct, Mr van Dyk?'

'Everything correct, sir. The only boys not at the sports, were the domestic servants. I think, sir, you should hear what Mr Wessels has to report.'

He brought in Mr Wessels, who reported that he had been on farm duty, and that while visiting the top portion of the farm, he had seen Sponono walking through the trees. Knowing that Sponono worked for me, he had contented himself with asking the boy where he was going, and Sponono had replied that I had given him leave to go walking on the farm. We showed Mr and Mrs

Anderson several of the photographs of the domestic servants, Sponono's among them, but they were unable to identify the boy who had menaced them.

'Bring Sponono here please,' I said to Mr van Dyk. 'Mr and Mrs Anderson, and Mr Wessels, I'll ask you to retire to another office.'

'This is the stone that the boy carried,' said Mr van Dyk.

'Please leave it on the table,' I said.

When Sponono came in, his attention was immediately attracted by the stone, but thereafter he kept his eyes away from it, by an effort of will, I thought.

'Where did you go this afternoon, Sponono?' I asked.

'I went to the sports,' he said.

'Were you there all the time?' I asked.

'The Principal knows I don't like sports,' he said, 'so after a while I went for a walk.'

'Where did you walk?'

He closed his eyes for more perfect remembering.

'Down past the stables,' he said, 'then down to the fields, then back to the pump-house, then back to the house, meneer.'

'Did you see anybody?'

'No one, meneer.'

Then Mr Wessels came in, and Sponono looked at him warily.

'Mr Wessels saw you at the other end of the farm,' I said. 'He asked you where you were going, did he not?'

'That is true, meneer.'

'But you said you saw nobody.'

'Not by the stables,' he said. 'But I did see Mr Wessels at the top end of the farm.'

'Did you see anybody else?' I asked. 'Think carefully before you answer.'

'Nobody else,' he said.

'Why did you tell Mr Wessels I had given you leave to take a walk?' I asked.

'I did not quite say that,' he said. 'Probably Mr Wessels did not hear me clearly, as I do not speak his language very well. I told him I was looking for something for the Principal.'

'For what?' I asked sternly.

Against his will his eyes went back to the stone on the table.

'Stones,' he said.

'For what?' I asked.

'For your garden, meneer.'

'I did not ask you to get stones for the garden,' I said.

'I wanted them for a wall,' he said. 'I was going to speak to you tomorrow.'

I pointed to the stone on the table. 'Is that one of the stones you found?' I asked.

He did not answer. The questions were coming rapidly, and he was finding it difficult to judge which of the possible answers were the least dangerous. He was breathing heavily, and he found it impossible entirely to conceal his distress.

'Why do you not answer?' I asked.

'You are frightening me, meneer,' he protested.

'I am only asking you questions,' I said.

'I can see you are angry,' he said. 'Something bad has happened, and somebody wants to blame me for it.'

'What has happened?' I asked.

'Something bad.' He would say no more. The sweat was pouring off his face.

'Leave us, Mr Wessels,' I said. I sat down at my table, but I did not look at Sponono.

'The boy Johannes was saved from prison, because you told me I was doing wrong. Is that not so?'

'Yes, meneer.'

'Now it is your turn to be saved from wrong,' I said. 'You will not lie to me, will you?'

In a low voice, he said, 'No, meneer.'

'You went walking at the top end of the farm?'

'Yes, meneer.'

'You were contemplating nothing evil,' I said. 'You were thinking only of stones for my garden. You did not wish to hurt anybody.'

'No, meneer.'

'But,' I said, 'a great temptation was put in your way. And before you could gather your strength, you had done something wrong.'

He was silent, and if ever a silence gave consent, it was this one.

'But now,' I said, 'you repent of what you have done, and would like to make amends.'

In the low voice he said, 'Yes, meneer.'

I stood up. 'Let us go and get the money,' I said. 'It will be a great joy to these two people who thought they would have no Christmas at all.'

We went out and got into the car, and he led me straight to the money, all sixty pounds of it. The Andersons were overjoyed, and Mr Anderson insisted on giving me ten pounds, and when I refused he wanted to give it to Mr Wessels, who naturally refused also. So he put it on my table, and I said I would send it to one of the Christmas funds.

'I feel almost,' said Mr Anderson, so full was he

with relief and gratitude, 'like giving something to the boy.'

'I understand your feelings,' I said drily, 'but I fear that the consequences of his act must be quite different.'

The consequences of Sponono's act were serious; he lost all his free privileges and was sent back to the security building, so that his term at the reformatory virtually began again. His offence was not reported to the police, because all reformatory offences except the gravest fell within my jurisdiction. Nevertheless he tried to get me to alter my decision.

'If I had run away and spent all this money,' he said, 'you would not have punished me more severely.'

When I admitted this, he said, 'What is more, meneer, I showed you where the money was hidden.'

'I am not a judge,' I said. 'My job is to teach you better ways, but I have not yet succeeded, therefore I must begin all over again.'

He could find no answer to this contention, so he said to me, 'I ask only one thing, meneer.'

'What is that?'

'I ask, meneer, that if I behave well, and if I again receive my freedom, I should be allowed to work again in your garden.'

'I am willing to agree to that,' I said.

'Is that a promise?' he asked.

I could see that Mr van Dyk was scandalized, but I smiled at him pacifyingly, and said to Sponono, 'It is a promise.'

He turned to Mr van Dyk and scandalized him further by saying, 'I am satisfied.'

Two weeks after that, Sponono had a fight with one of his fellows, and received a serious wound over the eye.

The doctor told me that the sight of the eye was impaired, and what was more, that when the wound was healed, the eye itself would not look very pretty.

We investigated the case carefully and came to the conclusion that both Sponono and his antagonist Tembo were equally blameworthy; but it was difficult to know how to deal with Tembo, for in a fight which had begun as a bout of fisticuffs, he had suddenly whipped off his heavy belt and struck directly at Sponono's face.

'What have you to say?' I asked Tembo. 'This is a grave offence that you have committed.'

'I know it is, meneer,' said Tembo. 'That is why I got permission to go to the hospital so that I could ask Sponono's forgiveness.'

'Did you forgive him?' I asked Sponono.

Sponono peered at me from under his bandages.

'I forgave him,' he said. 'He did not mean to hurt my eye. I might have hurt his eye too, if he had not hurt mine first. It was his bad luck, meneer.'

'You are a generous fellow,' I said to Sponono, 'and your forgiving spirit is an example to us. However, your forgiveness is between you and him; but between him and me is another matter.'

'You should find it easier to forgive him,' said Sponono, 'for it was my eye that was hurt, not yours.'

'You should have been a lawyer,' I said.

He smiled at me from beneath the bandages. 'Meneer, you are playing with me. I am not clever enough to be a lawyer.'

'Listen, Sponono,' I said, 'you may forgive a person, and I may forgive him, but that does not mean that he should not bear the consequences of his act.'

His one eye looked at me sceptically, as though I were

propounding a doctrine palpably false, but he was too polite to say so.

'Do you think,' I asked, 'that if a person is forgiven, his offence is wiped out as though it had never been done?'

'Yes,' he said.

'Tembo,' I said, 'you are dismissed with a reprimand. But your belt will be taken away from you, and a softer one will be given to you. If you will take my advice, you will not wear such a belt for the rest of your life, for your temper is hot, and will one day get you into serious trouble.'

Tembo said to me humbly, 'Thank you, meneer.' Mr van Dyk took him away, and I said to Sponono, 'Where did you get this idea of forgiveness?'

'It is the teaching of Jesus,' he said. He apparently had no idea of what I might be expected to know or not to know, for he added, 'Shall I get a Bible, so that I can read it to you?'

'No, you tell me,' I said.

'Jesus said that we must forgive those who offend against us, even unto seventy times seven.'

'Are you a Christian?' I asked.

'I am not,' he said. 'I am not good enough, but I like to obey the commandments.'

'Good luck to you,' I said. 'You may go.'

'Couldn't you forgive me now, meneer, instead of making me begin again from the beginning?'

'You committed a grave offence,' I said, 'for which I have forgiven you, but you must still begin again from the beginning.'

'Couldn't you forgive this much, meneer, that I could go now to work in your garden?'

'No,' I said. 'Not until you are free.'

He surveyed me out of his one eye, his learned superior who knew so little about the true meaning of forgiveness. What he saw was apparently discouraging, for he shrugged his shoulders.

'Why do you do that?' I asked.

'Because I see you are not ready,' he said.

I wished that Mr van Dyk could have been there, for he often thought I was ready to the point of foolishness. But I was denied that pleasure.

Two months later I took the decision to leave the service of the State, and therefore to leave the reformatory. I was obliged to give three months' notice and I tried to keep the news as secret as possible, but before long it was widely known. One of my first visitors was Sponono. His eye had healed better than expected, and had given him an incredibly knowing look; it remained half closed, as though he could have seen more of one's weaknesses had he opened it, but as though out of tolerance he would not do so, even though he would continue to give the impression that he knew all.

'I hear you are leaving, meneer.'

'That's true, Sponono.'

'You promised me,' he said, 'that when I was free I could work in your garden.'

'That's true,' I said, 'but I did not know I would be leaving.'

'Where are you going to?' he asked.

'I am going to Natal,' I said.

'I have never been to Natal,' he said, 'but I am sure I could work very well there.'

I was going to say, 'That is very good of you,' when he suddenly changed his tactics, and addressed me gravely.

'I did not regard your promise as merely a promise that I could work in your garden,' he said. 'It was rather a promise that I could be near you, and that was very important to me, because then I knew I would not get into more trouble.'

'You did work near me,' I said, 'and you threatened two innocent people with a stone, and stole sixty pounds from them.'

He looked at me as though he were pained by the coarseness and directness of my language.

'You said you had forgiven me for that,' he said.

'I have forgiven you,' I said. 'But I thought I should remind you that being near me did not help you on that occasion.'

I could see that he thought that the reminder was unethical. But he did not pursue the argument.

'When I am discharged,' he said, 'I hope I may come to work for you.'

'The people in Natal are Zulus,' I said, 'and you might not be happy among them.'

'I shall be quite happy,' he said with finality. 'There are many Zulu boys here, and I have not fought with any of them.'

'When you are discharged,' I said, 'if I am still in Natal, and if I have a garden, you may come to work for me.'

Sponono turned to Mr van Dyk. 'I am satisfied,' he said.

I glanced at my Chief Supervisor, but he looked quite non-committal.

So that was how Sponono came to Natal. He had not been there long before he told me that Cele, the gardener, was an idle and worthless fellow, and that Jane Zondi, who looked after our house, was a loose and dishonest woman. These revelations I bore with fortitude, but his next escapade was beyond reason. He had been invited to a party at Jane's sister's home in the hills behind the coast, and, dissatisfied with the food, had killed one of the chickens and made himself a feast. He had also drunk freely, and made advances of an ugly and threatening nature to Jane's sister's daughter. The whole countryside was up in arms against the stranger, and Jane's sister went to the police. The police came to see me, saying that it was difficult to obtain evidence in such cases, but that they had no doubt that Sponono had broken several laws; however if I would send him back to the reformatory, they would take no further steps in the matter. Jane Zondi also came to see me and asked me to build an extra room for Sponono in another part of the garden, while Cele asked me to buy another garden and install Sponono there as sole and all-powerful gardener, so that he could mismanage both the garden and his private affairs without involving others.

'No one seems to want you,' I said to Sponono.

'I can see that,' he said. 'From the time I came, they have all been against me; from the time they knew I came from the reformatory.'

'Who told them that?' I asked. 'It must have been you yourself.'

'Yes, I told them,' he said. 'I thought it would make them more patient with me.'

'The police say you have a choice,' I said, 'to go to court, or to go back to the reformatory.'

'These people hate me,' he said. 'It is better for me to go back.'

So Sponono went back to the reformatory, and so began my long correspondence with him, that has lasted now for ten years.

'Your action was very harsh', he wrote. 'Others at the party behaved just as I did. You must not think I was the only one who ate the chicken. Jane's sister's son ate just as much as I did, and he was the one who informed against me.'

He also complained bitterly against Jane and Cele, and said that they were of the kind that would never forgive any person who had done wrong, but would hound him down until he was destroyed. Furthermore they were Zulus, and hated him because he was a Xhosa. Also Cele was afraid of him, because it was clear that Cele knew nothing about gardening, and was afraid of losing his job to a better person.

'But you,' he wrote, 'you ought to know better. You have worked with thousands of sinners, and have gained a good reputation amongst us. Also you are a white man, and have no reason to hate me. Lastly, you are a writer, not a gardener, and you could never lose your job to a person like myself.'

When Sponono had served a further year at the reformatory, it was decided to release him, and he asked to be released to me. However, I declined to take him. I wrote to him and told him that Jane Zondi was still with us, and Cele was still in the garden, and neither of them wished to have him.

'They are unforgiving,' he wrote, 'but that should not be your nature. Do not be influenced by them. Do not be afraid to take me. Why should I make trouble in my own father's house?'

I fear that my nature remained unforgiving. I wrote to him that he had failed me twice, and had twice caused trouble in my house. I asked him whether there was not perhaps some fault in his own character.

'I have many faults in my character,' he wrote, 'but we are speaking of you, not myself. It is true I have failed you twice, but that is a long way from seventy and seven.'

'What can I do?' he asked. 'At one stroke you have taken away from me my home and my father.'

Now it so happened that I had a friend who was growing citrus in the Eastern Province. He was a tolerant fellow of the kind I had once supposed myself to be, and what is more, his employees were all Xhosas. With him I got Sponono a job, which lasted for exactly six weeks, when he was found guilty of stealing a jacket and money from a fellow-employee, and was sent to the prison at East London for two years.

'A useless fellow', my friend wrote to me. 'If you wanted to fire my enthusiasm for rehabilitation, why did you start off with such a quarrelsome scoundrel? He quarrelled with the other workers from the first day he landed here. His worst characteristic was that he was always reminding me of my paternal duties, which he claimed I had inherited from you. I should have thought that after your thirteen years at a reformatory, you would have known a bad egg when you saw one.'

'Your friend is a hard man', wrote Sponono to me. 'He had all your sternness but none of your good-heartedness. After all, I offended only once against him.'

Sponono was allowed to write one letter a month, and I was his correspondent. I sent him simple books to read, and he discovered that the Superintendent of the prison had known me when I was in the State service. 'I admire your letters to Sponono,' the Superintendent wrote to me, 'but I'm afraid your admonitions are wasted. He is a bad-tempered prisoner, and I have had to give him some spells of solitary confinement for fighting. Nevertheless, go on with the good work.'

'The Superintendent is a hard man', wrote Sponono. 'It is not like the reformatory here. There is no forgiveness for small offences.'

I do not know how this letter got past the eagle eye of the prison censor; in any event it was the last of its kind. For Sponono was due to be released, and again he asked if he could come back and work for me.

'Jane and Cele are still here,' I wrote, 'and they will not agree to your returning.'

'Who', he wrote and asked me, 'is the master in your house?'

It was some years before I heard from him again. This time he was in Tiger Vlei, a prison for seven-year prisoners, who might however receive quite a generous remission for good behaviour. He was allowed to write only at rare intervals, and I replied to him, but I must admit it was with a waning enthusiasm. For one thing the new Government of South Africa had made it almost impossible for Africans from one part of the country to work in another. For another, I felt that my relationship with Sponono had reached its end.

'You take a long time to answer my letter', he wrote. 'What is this change in you? There is no change in me.'

Nor did it look as though there ever could be. After five years he wrote that he was shortly to be released, and wanted to return to me. By that time I had moved to another part of the country. I was engaged in work that took me frequently away from home. I did not think of saddling my wife with the problem of Sponono.

'I cannot have you', I wrote. 'I still have Zulus working for me, and you do not like them. I do not think it would be successful.'

It was then that he wrote to me that he had always looked upon me as trustworthy, but that now I made him ashamed among his friends.

'Why have you turned?' he asked. 'You were always a man of your word, but now you have changed.'

'You do not say you cannot forgive me,' he wrote, 'but that is what you mean. But Jesus taught we must forgive unto seventy times seven.'

'I do not quarrel any more', he wrote. 'I have had a change of heart. So have you, but yours is in the wrong direction.'

Sponono, we have reached, you and I, what is called, in a game not known to you, a stalemate. You move, and I move, but neither of us will ever capture the other. I gave you your chance, and you would not take it, for reasons that are beyond either of us to explain. You gave me my chance, and I would not take it, for reasons that I thought sound and proper.

But I have no doubt that you wish, as I wish, that the game could have ended otherwise.

The Elephant-Shooter

I had been some years at the reformatory when young Richard Coetzee came looking for a job. He had been born and brought up in the hot bush of Komati Poort, and had a great knowledge of all kinds of wild animals. In fact that had been his real education, for he had idled his time away at school. Then he became an elephant-shooter for the Portuguese East Government. He was gay, serious, humble and cocksure by turns; his manners were those of a boy, but he must have been about twenty-five.

'Why did you give up elephant shooting?' I asked.

'I got sick of it, meneer,' he said. 'I got sick of shooting such huge beasts.'

'Why?' I asked.

'There's too much life in them,' he said. 'I can kill a small animal, that doesn't seem so bad. But in the end I couldn't stand bringing such big life to an end.'

'It's only a temporary job here,' I said. 'I've a man on six months' leave, and when he comes back you'd have to go.'

I told him how much money it was worth.

'I'll take it,' he said.

'Why do you want to come here?' I asked.

'I heard about your work, meneer. I thought it was a good job, more useful than shooting elephants.'

So of course I engaged him. He took to the work of the reformatory as a duck takes to water. The boys liked him and worked well for him. When it was half-time, he would tell them stories of the wilds, and they would have listened to him for hours, and sometimes they did, I think, when they were working on some remote part of the farm. Because he was only a temporary man, he had no fixed work of his own, but took out the spans of men who were sick, or on leave. Such rapid changes can be risky, as some boys will be quick to take advantage, but he seemed to understand them all, and nothing went wrong.

Yet for all that, he had the reputation of irresponsibility. He borrowed things like shirts and tennis-rackets without leave, and more than one angry staff-member complained to me. But when they were not angry, they thought he was a joke, and called him the Wild Man of Komati. He caught snakes and put them into his pocket, and then he would ask some boy to take out his handkerchief for him. He was always up to some kind of mischief.

He would come to see me often in the office, which he was not supposed to do, having his own immediate superior officer, Mr Robertson. But when he came he was so engaging that I hadn't the heart to reprove him. People told him he was currying favour, but he went on unabashed. He would consult me about this boy and that, and ask my advice, and then say to me with regret, 'If only I had a permanent job, I could do much better.'

'I told you I haven't one,' I said.

He would look at me sorrowfully, as though I did not fully realize my influence with the authorities, and go away shaking his head in deep dejection. One couldn't help liking him, but his reputation for irresponsibility grew. One day he took the meat from the mess and gave it to the dogs, saying it was unfit for human consumption.

He was very hurt when I made him pay for it, a large sum out of a small salary.

Then Neser left us to go to the mines, and it occurred to me of course that here was a permanent job for Coetzee. But his immediate superiors wouldn't hear of it. He had borrowed Robertson's car, and brought it back with the gears jammed, and had refused to pay for the repairs, saying that everyone knew it had happened before.

At that time we had arranged for each staff-house to have domestic servants from the reformatory. It was an ideal opportunity for some kind of training. But the choices were made so badly, and the exceptional freedom offered so many temptations, that this group, about forty in number, produced more absconders and offenders than any similar group in the reformatory. I was reluctant to give up the experiment, and was trying to think of some way to improve the situation. It was then that young Coetzee came to see me.

'I see the Principal is worried,' he said solicitously.

'Worried?' I said.

'About these domestic servants. Meneer, I have an idea.'

'Sit down,' I said. 'Let's have it.'

'The whole system is bad,' he said.

'Is that so?' I said.

'It's really so,' he said.

He was very diplomatic, and did not say, 'The Principal does this and that.' He said, 'They do this and that,' and invited me with a courteous but superior smile to join him in condemning them.

'They choose the wrong boys,' he said. 'They like a boy, and think he would make fine servant. But they are wrong. We mustn't choose boys we like. We must try another method altogether.'

'Is that really so?' I said.

He knew I was playing with him, but he ignored it. He was after a big elephant, and would not let a trifle turn him aside. And he knew I was listening.

'I have an idea,' he said.

'Let's hear it then.'

He looked at me calculatingly. He did not want to say outright that good ideas can't be thrown about carelessly, he just wanted me to see it for myself. He smiled at me secretly, half shy to be withholding the idea from me, half cunning.

'It's a good idea,' he said.

'I'll tell you if it's good,' I said, 'but I can't without hearing it.'

He fenced with me a bit longer, but he was growing uncomfortable. He felt I was using my authority unfairly, and he looked at me reproachfully.

'What are you here for?' I asked. 'To give me an idea, or to ask for a permanent job?'

He screwed up his face at the difficulty of the question.

'Have you taken this idea to Mr Robertson?' I asked.

'No,' he said. 'I kept it for the Principal.'

'Have you fixed up Mr Robertson's car?'

'I'm fixing it,' he said eagerly. 'He's too impatient.'

'Have you got any snakes in your pocket?' I said.

He had the grace to blush.

'It was a harmless snake, meneer.'

'A good thing too,' I said. 'Otherwise you wouldn't be here to tell me your idea.'

But he wouldn't tell me the idea. He just sat there stubbornly.

'Have you been taking fruit from the orchard?' I asked.

He was stung.

'That's a lie,' he said. 'Excuse my language, meneer, but whoever told the Principal that was telling a lie.'

'No one told me that,' I said. 'I just asked.'

He smiled half-heartedly.

'A joke,' he said. 'I didn't understand.'

'Now,' I said severely, 'we come back to the idea.'

Then I saw that he felt compelled to tell the idea, but the joy had gone out of it. And he had such a great gift for putting joy into his conversation that I relented.

'I won't ask about Mr Fichardt's shirt,' I said, 'nor about the hole you made in the mess roof to get the honey, so that the rain comes down into the bedrooms. I'll just ask for the idea, and I'll just tell you that I don't take a good idea without paying for it.'

He brightened up at once.

'It's a good idea,' he said.

'You've told me that before.'

'Meneer,' he said, 'they just choose any boy they like . . .'

'You've told me that too. Just tell me the idea.'

'Whenever a new boy comes to the reformatory,' he said, 'he goes to the new boy's span.'

'Agreed.'

'Then let the officer pick out those who are docile and obedient, and are likely to make good servants. Make a special span for them, and train them for their jobs, so that when the time comes for them to be made free, they will be ready for it.'

I listened judicially.

'Go on,' I said.

'That's the idea,' he said, disappointed that I hadn't known it.

'Umph,' I said.

'What does the Principal think of the idea?' he asked.

I saw that he looked a bit disconcerted, and as though he had shot his elephant, and in the right spot too, but the beast wouldn't fall. He watched me anxiously, waiting for the collapse.

'It's not a bad idea,' I said.

'Will the Principal try it?' he asked.

I looked very doubtful.

'I suppose I could try it,' I said.

He drew his chair a couple of inches nearer, as though he wished to talk confidentially, but in reality to look me over, to see where he would plant his second shot.

'You'll need the right man for it,' he said knowingly, 'someone who understands the idea.'

'That's just what I'm thinking,' I said.

His coolness deserted him, and he teetered about on the edge of his chair, wanting to shout out his name at me, hardly believing that a clever man like a Principal could be so dumb.

'Who is this Wild Man of Komati?' I said.

He didn't answer that, but looked very hurt.

'When will Mr Robertson's car be finished?' I asked.

'This afternoon,' he said. 'This very afternoon.'

'Then you get the job,' I said. 'Stop dancing about. And don't you say a word to a soul. I'm going to have a hard time with Mr Robertson.'

'I won't say a word, meneer.'

'You can go,' I said. I added menacingly, 'If I hear another word about . . .'

'I won't do it again, meneer.'

When he went out, I rang Robertson and asked him to come and see me. I was a bit aloof with him.

'About young Coetzee,' I said.

I could see Mr Robertson growing cold under my eyes.

'Young Coetzee?' he said. 'Sir, excuse me one moment.'

He was out of the office and back in a minute, and he poured out on to the table a box of chess-men.

'Look at these, sir,' he said.

I knew the chess-men, for Robertson and I had played with them more than once. They looked in pretty poor shape, and two of the knights had no heads.

'Count them, sir,' he said.

But I drew the line at that.

'What's missing?' I asked.

'Two pawns,' he said.

'Mr Robertson,' I said grandly, 'you and I are the pawns. Coetzee has got the job.'